Contents

GW00480745

ISBN 978 93 5300 855 0

Printed in India

The Old Man

One hot day in October I was in a small city in India on a client visit.

The trip from my hotel to the client's office had taken longer than expected. The auto drivers had recognized me as an outsider and the rates changed accordingly. Some tried to overcharge a flat rate while others demanded twenty rupees over the meter fare. The opportunistic behavior was understandable but I didn't approve being taken advantage of just because I was new to the place. I knew that if I waited a little longer someone would come along who charged the correct fare. The honest lot was getting rarer by the day and even frowned upon by their own kind. But thankfully they were still around.

So after my meeting, for the trip back to the hotel, I geared myself for the unavoidable. As expected, the first two autos were promptly rejected. It was mid-afternoon and the roads were not crowded. There weren't many people on that particular stretch of road.

I decided to walk and look for a busy crossroad where there would be more autos to choose from.

After walking for ten minutes in the sweltering sun, I noticed a bus shelter and decided to wait there for a while. I was surprised to find that unlike the usual bus stops this one was pretty clean and well maintained. It was the enclosed type with seats to sit and ample space to stand. The seats were three polished slabs of granite placed equidistance from each other. Three could sit comfortably on each seat. There was space to stand between the seats and the bus enclosure. Similarly, the space behind the seats could stand a few. There was a college campus right behind the bus shelter. The shelter was being maintained by the college, so said a banner. This probably explained its uniqueness. The advertising board above the shelter carried the name of the college with its courses offered. It was a typical marketing initiative.

Two women sat in the middle seat. The seat at the far end was not taken for a reason. There was a man sitting on the floor wedged between the seat and the enclosure. I took the empty seat on the other end. I was in no hurry and decided to take some rest. A bus stop on a main road usually attracted autos. I could catch an auto sitting in the shade. If not, I would walk after been refreshed. A bus arrived shortly and the women boarded it. Now the bus shelter was empty save me and the man.

When I had arrived he had smiled at me which I pretended not to notice. It was the city bred instincts of not paying attention to strangers, especially vagabonds. Moreover I didn't want to be hassled as I rested there. Though out of curiosity I would casually glance at the man.

He was around 70 years and medium built with a paunch. He had a worn- out face with its share of wrinkles. The wrinkles seemed to be more a signature of his economic condition than his biological one. His beard was white and his thinning hair barely covered his balding head. But for all his external appearance that said who he was, he seemed out of place. You see an expensive car in a poor locality and you know there is something wrong even though there is no logic to support it. An empty seat in a crowded bus, an unoccupied bench in a crowded station raises a red flag. These oddities get noticed without calling for attention. But you can't put a finger on it until you check it out further. The old man sent out similar signals. The face beneath the shabby outlook was clean. His clothes though worn out and torn near the shoulders were not dirty. Not filthy as one would expect of someone of the streets. It looked like he took care of his personal hygiene and regularly washed his clothes. I noticed that he sat on a rag and not on the floor as initially assumed. This was one fussy beggar! Maybe he was handling his OCD about cleanliness as much as he could.

He had a cloth bag beside him but no begging bowl. An odd thing was that he did not ask for alms from everyone. It was no big secret that a beggar asked money from everyone. It increased the chances of getting a few coins here and there. And they had no qualms about haggling people. This came naturally with the role. The practiced expressions of despair were delivered effortlessly. But it seemed that the old man had his own standards of begging. He was quite choosy about whom he asked money from. People walked on the road past the bus shelter even though there was a footpath behind it. It was as if there existed an inborn habit not to follow civic rules. The old man would closely observe people as they approached. As they came closer he would fold his hands and smile. The smile combined plea, despair, friendliness and sense of kinship with the fellow being. If the person looked he would say "Sister please" or "Brother please". No wonder his success rate was low. In the time I sat there, quite a few people had passed and only one had given him a coin. The coin had been tossed into his palm from afar.

But oddly he didn't seem to mind his low earnings. Maybe he had got used to it or had resigned himself to his poor begging skills. Anyone who scoffed at calling begging a 'skill' should observe them at work. The really good ones can buy your conscience with empty words and for your petty coin, sell you a moment of saintliness.

I spent the time watching people and vehicles go by. It had gotten hotter. Having sat down, I was now reluctant to walk in the sun again. It is only when you rest that fatigue and tiredness sets in. When you are busy in activity no matter how strenuous, it doesn't get noticed much. My decision of taking a break for a few minutes had broken the momentum. I wasn't gung-ho about walking up the road again for autos. I reasoned it was smarter to wait for the autos that passed by the bus shelter.

So as I sat there I observed the old man now and then. Curiosity had gained the upper hand over prudence. If he glanced at me I would look away deciding not to take notice of him. But his hopelessly inefficient begging was hard to ignore.

In a while a young girl entered the bus shelter. She had a scarf wrapped around her face revealing only her eyes. Without a pause she went and sat on the empty seat beside the old man sitting on the floor. I was surprised. Women took extra care around men in public places. They would rather stand than sit in any public transport if they didn't feel right about the man sitting in the adjacent seat. In some Indian cities buses had clear demarcation for ladies and men. At bus stops if there were only men standing inside the shelter, women would prefer standing outside it. This was taken for granted. But here was a young girl choosing to sit on a seat beside an old beggar despite the middle seat being empty as well. Now I was really intrigued. Had she not noticed him? Was she one of those pseudo free thinkers who, as a lifestyle statement, insisted on not adhering to the social norms? Or maybe she was plain naïve.

But I was even more surprised at what happened next. The old man and the young girl greeted each other with familiarity. They then proceeded to have a long conversation. I labeled the man a smooth talker who had a knack of building rapport as means of getting money. But there seemed to be equal participation from both. The conversation was what one would expect between a favourite uncle and his niece or a grandfather and his granddaughter. He would talk with a pleasant smile and nod appreciatively at her remarks. He would have a look of solemn concern while giving some advice. He gave her undivided attention while keeping an eye on the passersby. He didn't miss out asking alms to a suitable person. He wouldn't react to the snubs and continue his talk with the girl. Eventually her bus arrived and she left after exchanging pleasant goodbyes with the old man.

Though there wasn't much distance between the seats, I could hear only bits of the conversation. The girl's part was harder to fathom since she had her face covered and had sat turned towards the old man. I had tried hard to listen in without being too conspicuous. The gist of the talk in Hindi was this:

The girl was studying science in the college situated behind the bus shelter. She was contemplating whether to study further for her MSc or take up a job in the town. She was in the process of completing her final project, which she showed the old man, who remarked appreciatively. As was the case almost everywhere, her parents were keen on getting her married and getting the responsibility off their shoulders. According to them her studying ahead depended on her husband and in-laws. Moreover, they feared that if she studied too much, getting a husband would be difficult. The old man had nodded in understanding and voiced his own thoughts. He advised her to find a balance between her wishes and being practical in today's world. He suggested she take up some shorter course instead of a longer degree course. The short course should serve as a source of income. Marriage being unavoidable, he suggested that she listen to her parents' wishes but take her time to select a suitable husband.

By now I was truly amazed by it all. The old man was like a memorable character in a movie. Not likely to be seen in real life, but interesting enough to be believable. And the advice! People relied on self-help books or sermons by self-proclaimed gurus without hesitation. And here was a 'nobody' of a man who defied everything successful yet made a lot of sense.

After the young girl had left I couldn't help thinking of the permutations and combinations applicable to the old beggar's situation. Shortly after, a young man on a bike came up to the old man, greeted him and to my utter amazement handed over a Rs.20 note and rode away. The old man acknowledged this with a warm smile and folded hands. He then raised his gaze to the sky in gratitude.

This incident finally broke all my resolve and caution and made me want to know the old man better. I stood up and cautiously sat on the seat near him, albeit at the further end.

He looked at me and smiled. "Good afternoon," he said in English.

"Good afternoon," I replied automatically, wondering how to proceed.

"You are not from here. Which city are you from?" he asked politely in Hindi. He seemed to sense my discomfort.

I tensed and answered his question with my own. "How did you realize I am from a city?"

He smiled again. "You have all the traits of a big city - cautious, distrustful and self-conscious. But you are right in doing so."

"Look," I responded bluntly, wanting to come to the point, revealing yet another trait of a city-bred. "I've been watching you for some time now. I find you very interesting. So couldn't resist wanting to know more."

"Oh I see. I understand completely. After all I am a freak among beggars." He spoke proper English and with no malice.

"Umm. No. Not like that. I was just curious, that's all. I didn't mean to make you feel bad." He sensed my disbelief at his fluent English. He gave a proud but weary smile.

"No offence taken, Sir. May I request that we talk only in English? It's like rain in a desert for me."

"Of course," I agreed. "But I don't consider you a freak."

"Hmm. Sir....Let me clarify. Have you been to a circus?"

"Long time ago. As a child. Not sure if they even exist now."

"Yes." he agreed. "The old world is disappearing. So you must have seen the clowns with their funny painted faces."

"Yes".

"And they are expected to make funny faces and perform funny antics? People are supposed to laugh at them, right?"

"Yes."

"Any other image of a clown, Sir?"

It was like a teacher asking a student a question that he knows will be answered correctly.

"Ya. The clichéd one. A clown with tears painted on his face. A clown who makes people happy, but is really sad inside. That sort."

"Exactly!" He agreed with enthusiasm. His eyes had now lit up at the conversation taking place.

"Now imagine a clown who is not like this at all. What if this clown gives a speech instead of joking around? Nothing boring or complicated. Maybe something which the audience would relate to. How about an inspirational speech? Would it be accepted? What do you think? The audience would feel betrayed, no? They would think there is something wrong with that clown. He would be booed. And the other image? The one with painted tears? What if there is a clown who proclaims that he is happy outside because he is truly happy inside and is therefore the perfect clown. He would be resented by all! I am sure he might even lose his role as a clown. Both of them, Sir, would be freaks because they would not confirm to the rule. Just like what I am - a freak among the beggars."

He paused for breath. "I had noticed that you thought that I am not like the rest", he said with the gaze of a man who has seen life in all its forms.

"So you are a philosopher as well." I quipped, impressed.

He gave a sad smile "Philosophy is the balm of a suffering soul. When life gives you trouble in a large package, look closely and you will see a message at the bottom which says "Philosophy Attached." Philosophy is the candle holder to the candle of suffering. The trick is to have the candle holder last longer than the candle. If it is strong enough it will help endure anything, for the candle is destined to melt away. Yes, we are all philosophers. It only gets noticed in the light of the candle."

"I can't believe that you are what you are," I said sympathetically. I was reluctant to use the word 'beggar'. "So what happened to your life, Uncle?" The address had come easily. "Forgive me, but you are not even good at it. You haven't even got the basics right. Is it a recent compulsion?"

He looked away. I had probably opened a flood of memories. A couple walked by without him noticing them. They had given me odd stares. But by now I was too intrigued by his story to care.

He looked at me with life in his eyes. Words flowed effortlessly as he related his story.

"I come from a small village 25 kms. from here. We were very poor. Our only expectation from life was to be able to exist. My parents were uneducated but they encouraged me to study. I was a good student, you know? Somehow I managed to graduate. It was the biggest achievement for my parents. They were so proud. No one in our family had even attended school.

If you are born in poverty, to live a basic life is easy, as that is a step upward. When you've trained yourself to not want much then you don't get much. But since that is what you wanted, you are content and hence, happy. And getting no guidance made me ignorant of what life had to offer. So I took the first job offered in a small company in this town. Here I was lucky to meet people who stimulated me intellectually. I was respected for my work. My background or financial status didn't really matter to genuine people. My free time was spent learning and experiencing new things. One does not need a lot of money for that, you know - only access to the right source. I was content passing the years with my equally simple wife who – bless her – didn't demand much from life as well."

He paused. A sudden cloud of sadness passed over his face.

"When it rains it pours is the saying, right? Life turned into a thunderstorm of uncountable years. The company closed down. Failing to get a job after months of trying forced me to start a business which incurred huge losses. Shortly after this, my wife who was my biggest source of strength passed away. Circumstances finally forced me to sell everything I had and move into the shanty at the edge of the city. We assume that a decent educated old person would easily get shelter in the old-age homes run by charities. But it is not so easy. Charity homes are not always run by charitable hearts. People have their own purpose. Whatever that is.

I have been lucky to find a place in the poorest area here. I do not complain about it. I have a little bit of money. With that I can survive with just enough food and shelter for my short life ahead."

He stopped talking to catch his breath. He put his hand in the cloth bag to bring out a bottle of water. "Why am I begging here? We finally come to that big question that brought a humble me to your attention."

He took a few gulps of water, wiped his lips with his sleeve and put the bottle back in the cloth bag.

I waited, not wanting to say anything that might distract him from his train of thought.

"I live among certain type of people now. Tramps, beggars, labourers, hawkers and even prostitutes. I do not judge them for their work. Thankfully most of them are polite to this old man. There are other old people living there. But for all the life circumstances that are similar, I am as different from them as day is from night. And that is because I am just poor in money and not intellect.

You see Sir, I have always had a certain outlook towards life, which was nurtured by my parents despite our poverty. That inspired me to always seek education, not just a degree. It was a life changing mantra. A mind that has seen beyond the mundane needs to move further on. It cannot be drawn backwards. After a bird has experienced flight, it won't just walk on the ground however safe it might be. A one-winged eagle would rather crash into the trees flying than hop on the ground. Because that is what it is meant to do. And that is what my soul seeks.

My circumstances made me unsuitable for the society that I had got used to all my life. There was no one whom I could talk to. No stimulation of the intellect. No thinking beyond the physical needs of the body. What was I to do? Where could I find acknowledgment for who I really was? All I got was rejection for who I had become.

I even tried applying to NGOs. I thought I would spend my wasted life helping others. I had skills and the wisdom of age which could have been used effectively. But they seem to be closely related to the charity homes in their refusal to give me a chance. Reasons given were age, lack of experience in the NGO sector, no relevant qualifications. Maybe it was insecurity or reluctance to go off the prescribed norms. I don't really know.

One day I came across this bus shelter and an idea was born. Initially, I planned to just sit on one of these seats and chat up to anyone interested. But it is a crazy world. Even I knew that it would look strange and suspicious for an idle old man to sit here the whole day trying to talk to people. So I decided to be a normal part of the landscape. A beggar is an unwanted but integral part of any city. Along with garbage bins, hawkers, cobblers and *paan* shops, a beggar would be very much in place on a footpath. So I reluctantly became a beggar. The place was comfortable and just right. And because it wasn't exactly a lucrative location for begging, other beggars didn't feel threatened. I am sure they must have tried it here because no one objected when I took over.

I don't beg for the money, Sir. Any money is a great gift to me, I admit. But money is not what brings me here. All I want is a bit of conversation to nurture my soul. That is what I beg for.

I do not beg for the money. I ask for it. I request. And I totally understand if someone refuses or ignores me.

The money given is a bonus. It hurts more when someone actually gives me money than when they refuse. Because I become a beggar only when I accept the money. But I do beg for the right company and a healthy conversation. I do beg for those few moments when I can connect to my true self.

The college behind is the real reason for my presence at this bus shelter. Youngsters do not have the inhibitions that most adults do. Life has not yet coloured them. They are open to talk and are not conscious of being seen talking to me. Their talks make me feel young and alive. I get to share my stories, counsel them, and give suggestions. Quite a few use this chance to lighten their hearts. Once in a while I get clothes and food from these students, which mean more to me than the coins that are thrown."

He paused for breath and continued.

"I beg for my soul and not my stomach. I am ok with the 'beggar' tag because it labels the poverty of my circumstances. But the day the poverty reaches my soul is the day I will be really poor. Then there would be nothing more to live for.

I, Sir, am a beggar of conversations. I only ask for your time and words."

I took leave shortly after. My offer of money was politely refused with a smile of gratitude. He thanked me for listening to his story earnestly and for spending time with him. He looked a little happier as well.

The effect of the afternoon's events lingered like background music throughout the journey back to the hotel and a few hours more. Unable to shake off the incident and move on, I returned that evening to the bus shelter. Seeing me again, he was surprised but gave a welcome smile. I had brought food, a shirt and a bag containing basic necessities.

More important than these, I gave him a little more of my time. We had yet another wonderful conversation.

The Shop Boy

My engineering college was located in a small town in rural India. The town was within easy travelling distance to other small towns and remote villages. This made the college the preferred choice for students hailing from such places.

Having never seen a village except in movies I wanted to visit one. I had often wondered if village life was as shown in the movies. Mainstream cinema often portrayed villages to be picturesque and idyllic while art cinema overemphasized the struggles and exploitation. I surmised that only a visit to an authentic village would give the right picture.

A trip to Switzerland is usually a 'once in a lifetime' occurrence for many and having had the chance, they talk about it forever. Similarly, for someone more attuned to the urban lifestyle, a trip to rural countryside would be a novel experience. I resolved to make at least one trip during my college years to the remotest authentic village possible. It would be an experience to relate to my friends in the city. And I was sure that once I left college I would not want to return on my own accord.

A true adventurer would have hopped on any available local bus to any such place. But that was not me. So over the course of my years in college, I looked for viable opportunities through college mates and local acquaintances.

It was the late '90s. Millennium was round the corner and had become a buzzword in the cities. Out here, life chugged along at its own pace. Eventually with the final year exams we reached the end of a definite phase in our lives. Soon we would be returning to our homes.

I had increased my efforts in the final year to visit a village before setting off for home. A classmate finally invited me to spend a day with his family in such a village. It had taken four years of studying in the same class with me for him to be finally comfortable with this prospect. I grabbed the opportunity and along with my two eager friends we agreed to the trip.

The village was situated almost 70 kms. from the city. It might not seem very remote in terms of distance but in terms of accessibility, it definitely qualified. To reach the village by public transport one had to travel to the bus stand of a small town almost 50 km from the city bus stand, which itself was a half hour ride from our college. From this small town, you took yet another bus whose last stop was a junction connecting a cluster of villages. From this junction you reached your village by walking. The bus to this village junction would make the journey only twice a day. The bus arrived in the morning at around 9 am and in the evening at around 6 pm.

The twice a day schedule was because the route was hardly used. A majority of those who did, preferred a two wheeler – the sturdy cycle being the affordable choice. Even this commute was primarily to an adjacent small town, which served as their version of a city. Rarely was there any need to go to the main city. The bus to the village junction had been a routine development initiative by a local government department. The public had not been asked nor their views taken on its necessity. Because the bus existed, it was used without praise or criticism. If you missed the bus, you just shrugged and moved on. It was after all an unasked luxury.

The three of us reached the junction feeling every bit of the travel, where we were received by our classmate and his cousins. Wanting to give us an authentic experience right from the start, they had arrived in a bullock cart. It was a back breaking trip. We discovered new ways the body could be twisted. We held on to the sides tightly with both hands to avoid rolling off the back of the cart. The unpaved stony mud road increased the discomfort of the rickety ride. What should have been a pleasant ride ended up being a body aching excursion. If this was what 'authentic' meant I geared myself for the experiences ahead.

We spent the next day living up the life of a simple villager. The classmate's parents were farmers who owned the land. They cultivated different crops like sugarcane, tobacco and staple vegetables. The usual variety of trees and an exotic few were scattered around the place. Though not rich, it wasn't a poor household either. Popular culture often stereotyped the village farmer. Foresight had prompted the classmate's parents to educate at least one in the family beyond the minimum requirement.

However life was as rudimentary as one could get. The house was large enough to accommodate two families comfortably, with basic amenities. There were small light bulbs in each room with a table and fan in only one of the rooms. The men spent the day in the fields. There was no need to loiter about in the house. The chief stress for them, if one could call it so, was physical, which was channeled as a catalyst for instant sleep. Except during monsoon, the men slept outside on beds woven with nylon ropes. Undisturbed by nature and nocturnal noises they slept peacefully and woke up refreshed. Food was cooked on a *'choola'*, a mud stove that uses firewood. While the call of nature was answered in the fields, they bathed near a large open well and washed at a small pond a little further away. The women of the household were hospitable and friendly within socially comfortable limits.

All our adventurousness was consumed within the day. Having enjoyed this novel experience we were set to leave the next morning. I concluded that this was all I could take. Only those used to this way of life or who had a mindset for a rustic lifestyle would enjoy it beyond a day or two.

We woke up early, had breakfast and decided to walk the distance to the bus stop. We wanted to avoid the bullock cart and politely refused their offer of dropping us off on bikes. We didn't want to overstep the hospitality. We had around one hour to catch the bus on its morning schedule. We were in high spirits. Time passed planning future trips, pulling each other's legs and discussing previous days' highlights.

The path was scenic and we took everything in to reminisce on it later. Nature was present everywhere. It spread itself in all its freedom, unthreatened by concrete and man's greed in the name of development. In a short while we came across a sugarcane field where a friendly farmer offered us free sugarcane. Unable to resist we followed him through the field to a small clearing. We sat beneath the sky chewing juicy sugarcanes. To our delight the farmer brought a bag full of roasted peanuts. Our stay was prolonged munching peanuts and swapping tales. The jovial rustic atmosphere accentuated by fine weather added our reverie. It was after quite some time that we set out again with heartfelt thanks to the farmer.

Reaching the bus stop, realisation dawned that we were late. There was no one around. There should have been at least one or two waiting. After all the bus arrived only once in the morning. Absence of anyone meant the obvious. Looking at our watches for the first time that day, we saw that we were 45 minutes late. So lost had we been in the pleasures of the morning that we had not heeded the time. Indian standard time might be 'never-on–time' but we had underestimated it.

Words like timetable, schedule sounds sophisticated and are assumed to be the prerogative of the urbane. But every place has its own rhythm. Time had its place in the lives of the people here too. The business of the day might start late, close for the afternoon and stop late evening. The watch displayed the same time, but the concept of 'time' differed in people's minds. We had been ignorant of the way of the village and were paying a price for it. Cursing the lack of frequent buses and labeling it 'backward' was fruitless. It would only increase our frustration.

This bus would have taken us to the town from where buses to the city were available. Now the only public transport would be in the evening. We were stranded. We could either get a lift to the town or loiter around till evening. It seemed that our share of adventure was not yet over.

"Get ready to spend the night on the road today just in case we miss the evening bus as well!" one of my friends joked bitterly.

"Ok. I got my pillow." I indicated to a cluster of small stones. "And my bed is ready." I pointed to a slab of rock.

"Guys, this is no joke. It might really happen. Will *that* bus come on time? I will manage somehow. But what about you pampered *citywallas*?" Our local friend had spoken. I showed him the finger and took cognizance of the surroundings.

We stood in the middle of the road in the middle of somewhere. It felt like nowhere. The road was a small stretch of land between villages. One side had wild trees and rocky terrain. The other side was barren dusty land. There was a thin road running through this land which probably led to a village.

There was no one else around. To keep us company was a small rectangular tin shack some paces away.

We stood there for more than an hour with no success. People passed by in singles, in twos and occasionally, in threes. Villagers walked beside their cycle laden with load. It was the modern version of a donkey. Once in a while, a tempo would rattle by. Either there was no space or they were going in a different direction. The drivers apologized politely for their inability to assist us. We always offered to pay for the ride. But it was not about the money. For the local people, walking was the best and sometimes the only way to commute. Our desperation for a lift received amused reactions.

"The time you are wasting standing here in the heat can be used for walking", someone suggested helpfully. "And there are three of you. The time will pass without your knowing it. Yes, it is a long distance. But who said it has to be done in one stretch? When you get tired, rest under the trees. You will make it eventually. But by waiting here you will definitely not reach anywhere."

But we weren't convinced. The morning detour having backfired, we were in no mood for another adventure. The 'soon-to–be–Engineers' analysed that the time and energy required to walk the distance didn't make it a smart move. Even if we got a ride after a while, we would still reach earlier than if we walked. And that too with less efforts. Waiting at the bus stop for a lift required only patience.

By mid-afternoon the day had become hot. With our frame of mind the heat was much more unbearable. Not having anticipated this turn of events we hadn't carried any food or water.

The tin structure we had noticed earlier turned out to be a *paan* shop. It was situated strategically near the road. A few meters from it was the thin path which led to the interiors. Across the main road, diagonal to the shop was a street lamp which served as the unofficial bus stop. We hoped that the shop sold something to eat. There was no rule that a *paan* shop had to sell only *paan* and cigarettes.

The *paan* shop was managed by a little lad who gave an expectant look as he saw me approach. Anyone venturing to his shop was a potential customer. The boy was thin, around ten years old, barefoot, and had a pleasant face. He wore a faded T-shirt and shorts which ran till his knees.

I got the feeling that sitting in the booth, he had been observing us all this time. It was that sort of village - small enough that anyone not conforming to standard appearances stood out. Everybody probably knew everybody and his family.

The tiny booth had the usual layout of a *paan* shop template. Cigarette packs covered the wooden sides and *gutka* strips were strung at the front. A mirror hung in the centre, on one side of the square booth. Assorted tins containing *paan* ingredients were lined near the counter. There was a jar of menthol flavored candies - a must for smokers.

"Have you got any biscuits?" I asked in the local language. He pointed to one side without a word, conscious of my presence. Tucked away in a corner were the ubiquitous Parle-G biscuit packets. Something was better than nothing. I bought three packets.

"When is the next bus coming?"

"Gone." he murmured shyly. He had an innocent face.

"Ya, I know. When will the next one come? How do we go from here?"

He shook his head.

"Nothing for a long time. It will come here only in the evening. No one needs the bus at this time. So no bus is available. You can get a ride only if some tempo or truck passes by. Did nobody tell you this? Are you all lost? Whose house did you come to? They should have told you all this."

He was puzzled at our situation. The look also said *they all look the intelligent city types, supposedly smart. So how come they did this?'*

I gave a noncommittal shrug to brush aside his questions. I was in no way going to admit to this petty village kid that we had missed the bus due to our stupidity.

I walked back to my friends. The two had been standing in the middle of the road again. As if we wouldn't be visible in the emptiness of the surroundings. But no one wanted to take a chance.

There was a cluster of large rocks at the side of the road. Brushing the dust off with our fingers we sat to eat the biscuits.

For the thirsty, the first few sips of water are the elixir of life. It gives a feeling like no other. After the initial gulps the heavenly status of water reduces with each consequent sip and finally, it is just normal water. Likewise the first few biscuits were gobbled with delight and gratitude. It was a feast for the hungry. The biscuits that followed were munched indifferently.

Our hunger satiated, thoughts moved on accordingly. We realized that had we not missed our bus we would have been having a good lunch around this time. This made us all the more morose.

Like any other train, a train of thoughts usually connects similar compartments. A happy thought either heightens into exuberant joy or gradually reduces to feeling ok. This 'feeling ok', if not managed might lead to the links of feeling low which finally ends into deep sadness.

We were unsure of what to do. There was no visible solution to remedy a wrong decision. Our sullen thoughts led us to the bogie of 'feeling low'. Since there was nothing really to be sad about, our predicament slid into the section of 'uncertainty'.

Mind projections are either in the past or the future. Like a swinging pendulum the conversation moved between past uncertainties and future ones. After all, we were at the threshold of a new phase in our lives. It was the late '90s and millennium was touted to bring in great changes in the world. That is, if the world existed despite the doomsday predictions. Would we be ready for it? Were we ready for the next stage in our lives? We were to be designated 'Engineer' as per the certificate conferred by the University. In reality, the certificate was more an indicator of the years slogged at college than a qualification of being a skilled engineer. What value would this engineering degree hold in the real world?

"What do you want to be when you grow up?" a friend shouted at the sky. The silent thoughts had been aired aloud.

"To B.E or not to B.E?" I commented sarcastically. The joke was wasted on the two. One had not heard of Shakespeare at all and the other had, not surprisingly, only of *Romeo and Juliet*. I sighed inwardly.

We were reminded of that *big* question. The inevitable one that every kid in India has to encounter. A child who can speak and comprehend is deemed ready to face this question. It is usually in the presence of family members or friends. The kid is placed in front of the appreciative audience to perform - usually a song or a nursery rhyme. Then someone almost always asks the big Q. *"What do you want to be when you grow up?"* Any answer given is applauded because of the innocence behind it. But more often than not the impressionable kid has been unknowingly trained for it. For those growing up in the '80s the list was usually the same. Kids were influenced to say 'Pilot' for glamour effect without knowing what it entailed. Children are scared of going to the doctor so no one chose that, except maybe those whose parents were doctors. I had always wondered how come no one ended up saying 'Film Star', 'Item girl' 'Bus conductor', 'Waiter' or something out of the ordinary or mundane. Maybe they had done so in private. But the poor kid must have been hushed, reprimanded and trained for the right answer.

Growing up, the automatic answer to "What do you want to be when you grow up / what is your ambition in life / what do you want to do in life" had to be from the approved options. Topping it was 'Engineer'. Most of us didn't know what an Engineer did, even after completing school. Many couldn't spell it right. (How many 'e's in Engineering?) Yet we were supposed to aspire to be one. There was no way out for an ace student or one marginally good at studies.

So, we had become Engineers. But what next? The door to life's treasures didn't open with a key called 'Engineer', did it? Yes, there were those who excelled at it and knew what they wanted to do. But the majority did not. They were like the sheep sent to graze ignorant of the intent of their master. Was it for wool or meat? It did make a picturesque landscape though.

What lay ahead for graduates like us? We would start the hunt for a job and hope for a steady career. Some eyed the US via the MS degree route. If you asked them whether they were really keen on studying further they would give you the "Are you stupid or what?" look. The MS degree was a legal and respectable way of entering the US and settling down. Some others were planning for the current fad - MBA. But deep down most graduating students had no answer to "What do you want to do in life?" Yet, like a tradition kids across India had to face this question.

Such life goals dominated our conversation. We were so caught up in our emotions that we didn't notice someone sitting beside us. I turned and saw that it was the boy from the *paan* shop. He sat shyly with his hands clasped between his knees. It was probably rare to see college students from outside his village. Maybe there weren't many college students passing this way. Whatever the case we were curiosities to be checked out.

"What's your name?" I asked in a friendly tone. He was a timely distraction from our dreary topic.

He gave his name with a shy smile.

"Do you go to school?"

He nodded his head in affirmation.

"Which standard are you in?"

He raised his open palm.

"You can't speak?" my friend snapped in mock seriousness.

"Fifth standard," he replied sheepishly.

"What are you doing here then? Hooky from school? You don't like going to school or what?"

He looked down and shook his head.

"Aah! Good! You are normal then!" We all laughed.

We had regained our good mood. As typical youngsters do, we diverted our attention to the little lad. We decided to have fun. Time pass. We were in a playful mood. A part of us wanted to feel better after the self-doubting conversation a few moments ago. A natural tendency of man, a shallow being, is to look down at someone else to feel good about himself.

"Since you go to school you must know lots of stuff." one of us began.

"I think so," he replied hesitantly.

"So what is 6 X 7?"

The boy gave a blank look. "Don't know."

"Hmm. Ok. What's 7 X 6 then?"

Now he was confused. Thinking hard he said, "Don't know."

"What is the capital of Switzerland?"

No answer.

"Do you know where Switzerland is?"

Silence.

"Ok let this all go. Who is the prettiest girl in your village?"

Still no answer.

"Hey, do you know anything at all? Are you even sure of your name?

The boy nodded, affirming that much. He looked down at his feet. He fiddled with his hands not knowing what to do next.

The friendly teasing had lightened our mood. We decided to let go and free him of his torment. We stared at him. He had not looked up the whole time. His face was down in embarrassment. He was doodling in the dusty ground with a twig. He had refused the offer of biscuits. We weren't sure if it was shyness or the hurt feelings of a little boy.

"Ok cheer up," one of us said after a few minutes of silence. "Answer this one last simple question and we will stop bothering you."

The little boy gave a sideways glance at us waiting for the inevitable. He had no choice anyways. We looked at each other with knowing smiles. The question of questions! We mouthed '1-2 -3' silently and all three shouted in unison.

"WHAT DO YOU WANT TO BE IN LIFE!?"

He almost fell backwards in shock. We burst out laughing. One was laughing so hard that he had to wipe tears from his face. We were fully refreshed now. We weren't expecting any answer and decided to stop baiting him. We would buy him a chocolate from his shop as a goodwill gesture.

Suddenly the boy got up and stood in front of us. We were sitting on the rocks. We looked up at him. Had we offended him too much? We braced for a backlash from a little village kid.

But to our utter surprise he began shouting in excitement, "I know! I Know!"

What was wrong with him? We looked at each other in confusion. But he was grinning! He hopped in front of us in euphoria.

"Hey calm down! We were just pulling your leg. It was just fun. Don't take it to heart." I tried to pacify him.

"But I know!" he insisted.

"Know what?"

"The answer to the question!"

Now it was our turn to be confused. Was he trying to pull our legs?

"What question?"

He had a wild look of triumph.

"You all asked me what I wanted to be in life. I know what I want to be when I grow up! I have known it forever! But no one has ever asked me this before. No one ever bothers. No one cares."

There was bewildered silence from our end. He had not gone silly. Did this kid from nowhere want to play mind games with us?

"Ok Mr. Big Shot," one of us said mockingly "Tell us what you want to be."

But before he could speak we started.

"Engineer…"

"Doctor…"

"Pilot…"

"Film Star…"

"Politician…"

The richest farmer in India!"

"No! No!" he began waving his palms in exasperation. He had dragged us back to our mocking mood. We weren't going to let it go. But he hadn't noticed.

He stood with one arm pointing at something behind us. The look in his eyes was that of a sailor seeing a faraway horizon. Now that land had been located, hope and determination was all it would take to reach it.

Bemused, we turned to see what he was indicating. There was nothing except barren land. But he was pointing at something. It was the *paan* shop! What was in this boy's mind?

"That," he said with fervour, "is my goal."

There was spirit in his posture. Like the valiant heroes who see only their mission and not the dangers. Like the ambitious who are oblivious of the obstacles because their whole being is focused on the goal.

"I want to own that *paan* shop one day. I want to sit in one of my own *paan* shops. One day, I want my father to say that his son sits in a shop of his own. I want to *BE* the *OWNER* of a paan shop!"

We sat still unable to comprehend. He continued without prompt.

"That shop belongs to a '*seth*'. He stays in that town where you want to go. He is rich and owns lots of shops. He has rented out this shop to my father. We have to pay a fixed amount every day no matter what.

Anything above that is ours. My father also works in the fields whenever there is work available. Sometimes my mother also works in the fields with him.

I go to evening school. But only if my father can sit in the shop during that time. He then manages it till late night. I am not good at school because I don't like it. What will knowing about history, geography, maths do for me? I know how to count. That's enough. But I do know for sure that having money will bring happiness. I have seen how people respect money. There is even more respect if you have your own business. If you don't work for someone, then there is no reason to salute anyone, no? That is why I want to own the *paan* shop. Be the owner. Especially this one. My father started it and I have been running it with him for three years now. Some days we go home with profit and some days with loss. But we have nurtured it from nothing."

On the road behind him, a tempo laden with some kind of load was passing by. The uneven dusty ground forced the vehicle to move at a snail's pace.

But we made no attempt towards it. His story had us rooted. Our keen interest encouraged him to go on.

"I know that school will not help me achieve my goal. My evening school is not the same as day school. We are considered hopeless cases anyways.

Actual learning for me happens when I sit in the shop. I have learnt how to manage such a shop. I know how much it costs to own a *paan* shop. I know how much it will take to run it and make a profit. I know how to deal with people bigger and better than me. I have learnt not to let people treat me like a kid. I have learnt to detect when someone tries to take advantage of my age and cheat me. I have learnt to sell more than what the customer comes to buy."

We listened without interruption. It was our turn to look down at our feet. Could we escape by digging a hole in the ground?

But he kept talking enthusiastically; unaware of the effect his talk was having on us. He had an audience for the first time in his life. Such an opportunity might never come again.

"I have located other places in nearby areas where a *paan* shop can be successful. It's a secret. I don't want anyone else to put up a shop there. I know that you all won't tell anyone. There is a place I know 2 kms. from here. It is hilly with big boulders. People don't go there much. There is nothing to do there. But it is popular with couples and guys who want to drink. I know that this place will do good business. People smoke more when they are enjoying or are tensed. I know a few more places which generate such emotions. A *paan* shop there is guaranteed profit.

I want to be the one who has at least three *paan* shops in the village. One for me and one each for my parents. If I work hard I can do it. That is my goal in life. That is the only thing I want to do. That is what I do best."

He had finished talking but we were beyond thought or action. We didn't know why we felt so dumb inside. We looked at one another for moral support. Each waited for the other to regain our lost position. But no one knew how to respond. A condescending gesture of praise from our side would amount to filling that hole in the ground that we had dug in our minds, with muck.

Behind him we saw the slow approach of a trailer filled with brownish layers. The uneven road slowed down the vehicle. As it came nearer, we saw that it was filled to its brim with dried cow dung cakes. Was it symbolic?

The little boy had resumed his earlier demeanor. He was back to his shy self. Talking about his goals transformed him into a fiery avatar. Rest of the time, he was just another average kid. Maybe that's what true ambition did to a person. That's what made a hot air balloon soar - a focused desire to touch the sky. But what did we know.

The cow dung cake filled trailer slowly moved past where we sat.

The boy took his place on a rock beside me. As before his hands were clasped between his knees and body leaned forward. There was that look of childlike innocence and genuine curiosity again. With an earnest smile he turned towards us.

"You are all like my elder brothers. If you don't mind can I ask you all a question?"

Some instinct made us all get up at once, dreading what was coming. We looked towards the trailer having similar thoughts.

"Ask," one of us blurted without looking at him.

But even before he could utter the words, we had raced towards the trailer. We roared at the driver that we were going wherever he was going and before he could refuse, jumped on the cakes of cow dung.

Of course we could not avoid hearing the question. The boy, surprised at seeing us dash ahead had shouted, "WHAT DO YOU WANT TO BE IN LIFE?!"

Never had a ride been as inviting as that on a cow dung filled trailer.

The Hotel Family

It was around 11 am that I found myself waiting at a bus stop for a ride out of a small town. As a Regional Sales Manager my territory encompassed minor towns within the allotted region. The state transport bus arrived. I was lucky to get a window seat. My destination was yet another town a few hours away.

About an hour or so in the journey I noticed a medium sized business premise with shops and offices. Without a thought I alighted at the nearest bus stop.

A true salesman is always alert for any 'out-of-the-way' opportunity. A new sales call might result in a potential customer and contribute to the monthly revenue targets. For sales professionals, a foot in the door is a window of opportunity. A visiting card or a brochure is like the toe in the door. Just two of the offices turned out to be prospects. It was better than nothing. I walked to the nearest bus stop to resume my journey.

On asking around I was told that the next bus would be only after two hours. It would arrive around lunch time and reach my destination by tea time. The thought of missing lunch made me hungry. I decided to look for a place to eat not too far away. It would be a productive use of the wait.

I walked along the road in front of the bus stop. Up ahead I saw a cooler at the entrance of a shop, painted in the colours of a soft drink brand. This was a sure indication of a hotel or a grocery store. On approaching it I saw that it was indeed a small hotel. To my surprise there was a big hotel right next to it. They shared a common wall. But the difference between the two was like chalk and cheese. The bigger one was like any other standard restaurant. It had a huge neon signboard gaudily calling attention to itself. Below the sign 'GRAND HOTEL,' was written 'South Indian, Punjabi, Chinese Special.' A sticker on one window stated 'A.C Family room'. A bike was parked outside the entrance, probably that of a customer.

The neighbouring hotel was a total contrast - simple, bare and almost invisible. I didn't see any apparent signboard indicating it was a place to eat. There was no customer as assumed by its empty front. No advertising at all to lure customers in.

As a marketing professional, it went against every grain of business logic. So I can't explain why I entered this hotel and not the better looking one. It wasn't curiosity. It was probably because it was the first one in my path. Had I come from the opposite direction I might've probably entered the bigger hotel. But that's speculation.

When one walks with a purpose there is a certain pace to the stride. It is only when we reach our destination that we pause. As my mind opted for the simple eatery the momentum carried me beyond the threshold and into its confines. The setting was roughly divided into separate areas. The entrance area had the refrigerator which I had noticed from the road. An elevation of a single step led to an area occupied by four tables. Each table had two plastic chairs each on opposite sides. They were all empty. Further beyond was a counter separating the back end of the place. This served as an open kitchen. There were huge vessels and cooking essentials.

Utensils covered with lids were lined to one side. A youngish couple stood in the kitchen.

The man was in his early thirties. He was tall, medium build with a mustache and stubble. He wore glasses and his hair, white at places indicated maturity beyond his age. He had a simple demeanor. He came across as a school teacher. No one would have guessed he ran a hotel business.

I presumed the dusky slim woman wearing an apron over a saree was his wife. She gave a polite acknowledgement and returned to her work. The man had been surprised to see me enter. Any customer choosing his drab joint over the fancy one right next door probably deserved such a reaction.

For a moment I doubted my decision. Someone of a firm nature would've taken the stance of 'my- money-my–wish' and left the place. But I avoided awkward situations and took care not to embarrass others. The couple had already acknowledged my presence. So I decided to stay and see what was on offer. In the worst case scenario I would have a soft drink and leave.

I sat at one of the tables. The man quickly came over and stood beside me.

"What have you got?" I asked, not seeing any menu around.

"Welcome to our place Sir," he began politely. "Sorry but we make only limited stuff. Items preferred by locals." He had noticed my looking around for a menu and explained its absence.

"No problem. So what is there to eat?"

"For today we have *lemon rice, puri, bhaji, idli wada* with *sambar*. There is *sheera* and *pakodas* for snacks. There is tea and coffee to drink. Or you can choose any of the cold drinks in the cooler."

I opted for the simple lemon rice and bottled water. If it tasted satisfactory I would eat something else. There would be no food till dinnertime.

"Very well Sir. Please excuse us if the service takes longer than necessary," he apologized in advance.

"No problem. But don't take too much time. I have a bus to catch."

He nodded demurely and walked back behind the counter.

Within seconds there was a little boy at my table placing a glass of water. I had seen two kids on entering but not paid much attention to them. My mind had been busy judging the place. Now I took in the scene at leisure.

The two kids, a boy and a girl, appeared to be of the same age, around 8-9 years old. They might have been twins though I couldn't really tell. Many siblings look alike in their childhood. The girl was bespectacled. She looked studious. She had a maturity far beyond her age just like her father. She sat cross legged on a plastic chair. The table in front of her served as the billing counter. On it was a receipt book, calculator and some books. The girl was immersed in a book.

The little boy was shy and didn't look up often. His gaze was mostly directed at the floor. Apparently one of his duties was to place glasses of water at the tables.

It seemed as if the children were being trained at that tender age to run the hotel. Was it by necessity? Was it to instill business acumen at an early age? There were business families who believed in this philosophy. Whatever it was, it gave the impression of a close knit family who worked and played together. The atmosphere was pleasantly casual. There were no unnecessary pretenses of the hotel business. The lemon rice that arrived was tasty and complemented the homeliness of the place. I was sure the family too ate the food cooked there.

I ate the food with relish and it must have been visible on my face. Knowing fully well that I had liked their food, he came over and asked, "How is it, Sir? Are you enjoying it?" I gave him a nod of appreciation.

As the plate was taken away by the boy, the girl took out the receipt book for the bill. I couldn't help being impressed by the silent efficiency of the young ones. I smiled at them. They smiled back shyly and looked at their parents. The mother stood at the counter on the side of the kitchen. Seeing her kids being appreciated she smiled with pride. Taken in by the whole scenario,

I decided to reward them. I ordered some *pakodas* for myself to increase the bill amount.

I gestured to the girl to stop making the bill. To her father I asked, "Can I have some *pakodas*? Will you get it packed so I can take it with me?"

The man beamed with happiness and looked at his wife. I sensed the reason for it too. It was not so much the bonus money. He had sensed my initial reluctance — I looked the kind who would have normally preferred the hotel next door. My additional order was a vindication of their good food and good service.

"There are *pakodas* already made in the morning. But I will give you fresh ones Sir. It will take only 15 minutes. If that is ok with you."

I agreed to wait. There was more than an hour for the bus to arrive. Sitting there was preferable to standing in the hot sun at the bus stop. The man went over to tell his wife to cook fresh *pakodas.*

Observing the kids again I couldn't help admiring their sense of responsibility. At their age, how many kids were well- mannered at a hotel, let alone assist in running it? The kids when not busy in some chore, would be studying. The little boy had been given the task of getting the parcel ready for my *pakodas*. He was carefully wiping half a banana leaf with a wet cloth. Beside him was a large square shaped butter paper which he would place on this leaf. This would be given to his mother to put the *pakodas* on. There was a small paper box and a thin plastic bag to finally hand it over in. The girl was ready to write in a notebook filled with columns. It was probably all the items I had purchased - to be added to the day's business so far.

I was so engrossed in watching them that I didn't realize when the man had sat at the adjacent table. Watching me watch his children, he smiled with that familiar sense of pride and said "Bhuvan, Sir."

I acknowledged it politely without really understanding what had been said.

With a smile he indicated his children, "My son - Bhuvan. My daughter - Bhuvani."

"Oh I see. Good." I responded. "Very good children. Very smart." But this was not the response he was looking for. I was surely missing something. What was he expecting me to grasp that failed to get my attention? I looked at the kids again. Was there something about them?

He continued looking at me with an expectant smile. I was getting a little conscious.

Helpfully he continued," "My son is Bhuvan - you know…... And my other is a girl - so Bhuvani."

I realized then that it had to do with the name. It wasn't a common name so why did it feel familiar? My mind furiously worked to dig out a connection. There was a lot of stuff in it. It was taking a while.

Bhuvan? Bhuvani?

And then it struck. It was from a movie!

It was the name of the character played by Aamir Khan, a film star, in his movie 'Lagaan'. It had been a massive hit and nominated for an Oscar. It is one of the best inspirational Bollywood movies. The impact was such that the movie became a case study on motivation and leadership at B-Schools. It told the story of how a bunch of simple villagers led by

Bhuvan took on the haughty British officers in a cricket match challenge to get back their land.

"Oh I see! Bhuvan from Lagaan!" I exclaimed finally. The man beamed at my recollection.

"So you are an Aamir Khan fan? Do you like his movies so much?"

"Aamir Khan is a good actor. Big star. But I am not a big fan of movies. So – so fan."

"Then why …? " I asked bewildered.

"The movie, Lagaan. It changed our lives. We rarely see movies. But we saw this movie at the right time. It has transformed our life."

Movies, songs, books have always made an impact. Famous people sometimes talk about how a certain movie or a book made them follow a path that brought them success. Lists like - 'most inspiring' or 'most motivating' are common. 'Feel good' lists of movies, music and books provide us with that momentary rush. But a lifelong transformation was a new discovery for me.

I was intrigued and amused. I judged this couple to be naive and gullible. Some people believe everything they read or see in the media. Such easy targets are a favourite of the marketing world. Let a well-wishing maid / driver / watchman suggest a good product and it will be scoffed at. It might not be chosen at all just because it was suggested by them. But people will buy the same product if advertised by a film star, even though they know that it's all a media created 'larger-than-life' persona. Though unknown personally celebrities were so well-known publicly that they praised products for a price with rehearsed sincerity.

Were this couple so mesmerized by a movie to name their kids on a character? A few hours of entertainment would now last a lifetime in this household!

We could hear the sizzling of the *pakodas* as they swished about in the hot oil. It would be a while before they were ready. Taking a cue from that, I decided to continue this thread – a force of habit. A still salesman is a dead salesman. A good sales professional is one who is either talking or listening to people - engaging them in a conversation. A great salesman is one who does the listening more than the talking. So encouraging him to talk, I listened.

He turned to me. The kids were reading but their attention was on us. It felt as if his wife too was aware of what was going to be said. The life story of the family was being laid across the table in courses.

"My grandfather and his two sons," he began, "were simple tailors in this town. It was our family profession. They made enough to sustain the joint family on a simple lifestyle. As it usually happens, after my grandfather passed away the two brothers parted ways. They were now friendly competitors in the same town. Customers got distributed as per rapport. My father was good only at his work and not business. And he saw no future as a tailor for me. So he encouraged me to study so that I could get a secure government job. Which I did. Unfortunately the job was in a neighboring town 20 kms. from here.

During our good phase our united family bought some land at a very cheap rate. At that time the plot was considered useless. It was at the edge of the town with nothing around it. Eventually a road was constructed to connect neighbouring towns. Luckily this road passed along our land. And so the value of our land increased. This hotel and the one next to us are built on that land.

Initially the family had constructed a common shed over the plot to prevent any land grabbing. At that time no one had any idea what to do with it so it was left as it is. The joy was in owning a piece of land in our own town. Not everything is about making money, you know.

My cousin, that is, my uncle's son, is a tailor in the town centre. Within just a year of his father's demise he decided to make easy money by selling his share of the land. This was a few years ago. My father had passed away earlier. All my pleadings not to do so were shrugged off. As per him I was not staying in the town anyways. We were not very close. So there was no strong bond. We had to divide the land by partitioning the whole shed. There was nothing I could do. I had been married for only a year and had my own responsibilities."

The man had talked at a stretch, almost afraid that he might be interrupted. Pausing for a break he looked at his children. I could see that he was garnering strength from them for the tough part of the story ahead.

"Greed and need are sometimes similar - like salt and powdered sugar. You recognize it only after tasting it. A really needy man is greedy for minimum salvation. And a greedy man always needs more."

I nodded in agreement. That was something to ponder over with my sales team.

"My cousin was greedy for a fast profit. There were offers for his share from our town itself. From trustworthy people. But he was so obsessed with money that he chose a buyer based on what was offered. Can you believe that the businessman offered him only Rs. 50,000 more than the others? I tried to reason with him but he taunted my 'intellectual "attitude. He is not educated you see. And I am a graduate. I think that's also one of the reasons he resents me.

This businessman fellow is from a big town nearby. Somehow he developed an interest in this place He was very keen on buying it. Maybe he had inside knowledge of the road coming up. He knew there was big money to be made.

He is like those cut-throat businessmen we hear about. Not a bad man or a criminal in that sense. But who believes that the end justifies the means. After acquiring the portion next door he started leaning on me to sell my side as well. He wanted the whole area. He would send people at regular intervals to my house and office. Sometimes it was with offers of money. Sometimes it was with so called 'inside information' that the government planned to buy the land at throw away price to expand the road.

He claimed he was insistent only because my plot was lying unused. He knew I was not the kind to start a business nor would I leave my secure job. I lived in a far enough town. I feared for my unsupervised land here. When one day a part of the partition wall collapsed 'by mistake', I knew something had to be done before I lost it all.

Sir, for people around here their piece of land is a precious possession. There are values attached to it. For some it is the status of a landowner. For some it is about the tradition of handing it over to the next generation. You know. That sort of thing.

After the wall collapsed my only goal was to defend the family land. Nothing illegal had happened till then. So where could I go to complain? What would I say? The only solution was to counter his reasoning. Since the man claimed that he was only interested in my place because it was empty, I decided to make use of it. But no one in the town wanted to rent it. No one knew what to do with it. I didn't want to rent it to strangers from outside the town. I would have had double trouble if things went wrong.

The only way out was to start something on my own. But even I didn't know what to do. I had no professional skills. The whole idea behind studying and getting a stable job had been to avoid this very thing.

After a few months of wondering we decided to start a small eatery here.There are already two hotels in the main part of the town. We know that not many would come to this area just to eat. There are bigger hotels in nearby towns within driving distance. But this was the closest option to what we both could manage. My wife is a good cook as you know by now. It is still considered a woman's domain around here. But even I love cooking and help her wherever I can. We cook only a few items which are preferred by the locals. No special Chinese Punjabi dishes. We decided to stick to what we know best. The food would be simple and affordable. So you see, Sir, we had it all planned. It sounded like a good idea."

He paused, lost in thought. By this time the little boy had come and sat in his lap. The little girl brought a glass of water for her father and quietly sat beside him. Conscious of social decorum the wife had taken a seat in the kitchen. She listened to her husband relive their lives. The steaming *pakodas* were waiting to get cooled. In the silence of his pause only the whirling of the fan could be heard. I dared not say anything lest the momentum was broken and he realized that he was opening their whole life to a complete stranger. He continued after regaining his composure.

"By then it was almost a year since my cousin had sold his share and started this turmoil for me. His plot had not yet been used for anything. It was lying empty

- as if waiting for the other half to make it whole. But we had at last found a solution. We believed he would stop the pestering after learning of my plans for a hotel. After all, wasn't that the reason he had been giving me? But he tried to talk me out of it with his usual slimy sweetness. He explained in details the dangers of the business and the heavy losses that incur. I knew then I was on the right track and stayed firm. Finally he gave in and wished me well saying that 'his doors were always open'. All honey dipped words of false goodwill.

We started winding up our lives in the town where I was working. It took time but we were in no hurry. We were sure the issue was solved. My wife was pregnant. We had a lot to do for the future."

The man took a long breathe clutching his boy closer to him. His pained expression spoke of rekindled memories.

"We heard rumours about construction work on the neighbouring site. Within a month the place had become the hotel you see now. We were shocked. What could we do? There was nothing wrong about it.

But the man had taken advantage of our good faith. We had forgotten how cunning he was.

We were at a total loss. How does one compete with a big hotel right beside your small eatery? We were not sure if it was sensible to even start one now? Cooks, waiters and the manager are from outside our town. So there is no chance of any local affiliation with us. And you can see the advertising and their facilities. On our own we would have stood a slight chance. But in direct comparison we would come across as low grade. There would be no chance at all. You too had doubts, no?"

I shrugged as he continued.

"The value of this place has increased. But it is still not an ideal location for a hotel. And definitely not for two. This is a small town. People drive past it. No one comes here except those who have family. The flow of outsiders is very less. There is low scope for a hotel business here. So it was obvious why that that hotel was set up. His plan was to scare us into not starting our eatery. Then he could resume the same old tape. Even if we started one no way could we compete against the big hotel. He was sure that we would close down with heavy losses. That would make it even easier to ask for my land. Maybe even at a reduced price. It was a no-win situation any way we saw it.

We were very disheartened at that time. There was no regret in giving up my job because the land was priority. My family honour was at stake. But there was nothing to sustain us and hold on to the land as well. We thought of everything possible but no idea seemed right. With a heavy heart we would see the hotel go about its daily routine. The initial months saw a good crowd. People came out of curiosity. But soon the numbers reduced. But that was no solace to us, who had nothing.

One day we decided to just forget our worries and enjoy ourselves. My wife was 8 months pregnant at the time. The best option was a movie. We have only one movie theatre in our town. There was no choice but to see what was being shown. Fate must have decided to come to our rescue. The movie was 'Lagaan.'"

He looked at his wife. The lingering look was a story in itself. It told a tale of togetherness. It spoke of all the tribulations of the past years. It acknowledged their grit and their survival.

"Everyone was talking about this hit movie. We didn't really care. We are both not movie fans. And by then we had neither time nor money for such luxuries. The intention was to just lose ourselves for a few hours. But the movie had such an impact on us! I can't explain it in words. It was as if it was made for us. It was telling us how single handedly the hero motivated the villagers to fight the unjust officers on their own terms. You have seen it Sir, so I don't need to tell you the story."

I nodded as some scenes flashed in my mind. He beamed understandingly and carried on.

"We saw it again the next day. And the next. We saw it for four days in a row! We felt it was sending us a sign. A message! Just like in the movie, we could motivate ourselves and find a way out. We could do it with what we had, instead of waiting for the right opportunity. But more importantly ..."

He faltered, his voice suddenly breaking.

"The most important message the movie gave us was – 'learn the skills and beat your rival at his own game'! Do you see, Sir? Beat him at his own bloody game! Like cricket in 'Lagaan', I realized I had to defeat my tormentor only through the restaurant business."

He was so overcome with emotion that he looked away to hide tears. His wife came over and silently put her hand on his shoulder. Within a moment he composed himself and apologised. He was relieved that I had pretended not to have noticed his loss of composure. I asked him to carry on as he took a sip of water. Encouraged by my genuine interest he continued.

"Sir, our mindset totally changed in those four days. We resolved to start our eatery no matter what. We decided to follow our instincts and see what happens. We would keep it simple, watch the expenses and work hard."

He smiled affectionately at his children. Then he looked at me keenly.

"Sir, have you ever eaten food with so much concentration that you are totally immersed in its taste? If you have, then you know that thinking of it or calling its name will bring the same sensations to life. It is possible - trust me. But we have too much on our minds to be really focused on the moment. By the fourth viewing the movie was within us in mind and spirit. We no longer needed to see the movie to get inspired. To get the essence of it we just needed a signal."

He gestured towards his two children.

"Our symbols of inspiration – our twins. They are our life changing mementos. They are a double dose of magic. We named them Bhuvan and Bhuvani after the hero in 'Lagaan'. Their presence refreshes our renewed spirit.

The kids stay with us whenever they are not at school. Today is a holiday. They are here because we both work here all day. As they grew older they started helping out. This is not the future for them. But this is their present and they have to do what it takes to preserve it.

It has been more than five years now since we have been running it. It took us almost a year to start the eatery. We make enough to sustain ourselves. We concentrate on the few things we know and give it our best efforts. Our main source of revenue is home delivery orders. Many people prefer our homely food to the hotel stuff. One cannot eat *biryani* everyday but one can eat lemon rice. It's an advantage to have grown up in this town. Everyone knows the story behind all this and are happy to support us. We also have the contract for the midday meal at our local school.

I am aware that it is a very small a set up. Only so many tables fit in here. But what is important is that every one customer coming here is one customer less at his place. Every parcel delivered at home is one less hungry person who might have gone to that hotel. There is an understanding with the two hotels in our town to work for mutual benefit. We recommend customers between us and even assist one another on special occasions. I have always maintained good relations with my home town. This goodwill is paying off.

The man is so obsessed with winning the war that he is losing the battles. One day these battles will not be worth the war for him. I know it. We have learnt enough of this business to know that the overheads are getting harder for him to bear. He is the mighty tree which can be toppled over. We are the grass - always rooted to the ground. You can trample us but we will not break."

He exhaled audibly and stood up. He gestured to his wife to get the *pakodas* packed.

"That Sir, is the story behind Bhuvan and Bhuvani. I hope I have not taken much of your time. Please come again if you ever pass this way. Thank you for spending time with us. Please don't mind if I refuse to take money for the *pakodas*. It is a gift from the family."

"No. No." I refused politely. "I will not take it for free. And now I will relish it even more. But please let me pay for it. Thank you for sharing your story with me. Maybe there is something in it for me to learn too. Can I buy chocolates for Bhuvan and Bhuvani?"

He gave in to my request with gratitude. I paid for the food and the chocolates. The kids thanked me with shy smiles. Bhuvani promptly sat to note down the expenses in the notebook.

With good wishes for the future I took my leave. Later in the bus I reached into the bag to eat the *pakodas*. There was also a receipt in it. I had not noticed it till then. I glanced at it admiring the family's resolve. The receipt had the name of the eatery which had escaped me all along. It read "*LAGAN*" which meant 'perseverance' in Hindi.

The Beggar

He was a cynical man, always grumbling about the declining values of society. The media did its bit to add fuel to his agitation with the kind of news it splattered. The pet peeve in his baggage of complaints was the increasing filth in the city. His idea of a great nation was a clean nation. It was not just places and environment that were to kept clean . Society had to be rid of those elements that added no value to it.

He despised people who didn't work for their living. They were not positive inputs to society. People who depended solely on others without a valid reason were deadwood. Beggars topped his hate list. In his opinion even prostitutes were a better lot because they worked for their money.

His rant about beggars was exhaustive and exhausting. Beggars were the ultimate free loaders of the society. They were parasites who didn't contribute to the city in any way but only enhanced the dirt factor. While the disabled deserved some consideration, the able bodied were not worth being pitied. They would pester you for money at strategic junctions of the city. They understood economics better than a lay man. A rupee was not worth accepting. A haughty beggar at times would not hesitate to throw the coin back at you! It had to be at least a two rupee coin. Talk about the rules of alms giving!

Women were the most efficient of them all. Many a woman would have a baby (usually rented), bawling in her arms and sometimes a kid at her feet. She would plead for her children's sake. Female target were vulnerable. Their maternal instinct would take over their common sense.

It irritated him to see this tribe even if they did not approach him. If they did, he would studiously avoid looking at them. If they lingered longer than his stipulated tolerance limit (1 second) the unfortunate beggar would receive a lecture peppered with abuses.

Any soft-hearted soul, unlucky to be around him when giving in to a beggar was not spared either. "It's because of people like you that they exist," he would scold. "No one will starve to death. If they don't get alms they will be forced to work for their food. Even stealing involves hard work. But why should they bother when they have ready ATMs at their disposal." Of course, no one paid any attention to him. The beggars were immune to such minor "occupational hazards". And people were selfishly concerned about their own 'good karma'.

Once when he was in an auto at a traffic signal, a beggar boy approached him. Instantly irked, he brusquely asked the kid if he was ready to work if given a job. The boy's response was a smirk and a quick move to a couple on a bike. The auto driver gave him a "what – a naïve – man" look. "*Saheb*," he said "don't waste your energy. Your good intentions are not good enough for them. The boy has been given only this side of the traffic junction. But do you know his daily earnings? Rs.100 a day at least! Imagine festival days when people are in a generous mood. And *Saheb*, he has two brothers and a sister on other sides of this junction. The kids hand over the coins to their mother as soon as they get it. She sits like a queen under the flyover. She is well dressed with lipstick and all. You should see her. Gold earrings, full bodied. Aren't these signs of prosperity? You would never imagine her as a beggar."

Such incidents were stacked in his memory for ready reference whenever he needed an excuse to rant about beggars or justify his outbursts.

It was a routine day when he set out from his home in one of the middle class suburbs of the city. He had taken voluntary retirement from his job at a bank and now worked part-time in a small financial firm. This was an avenue to pass time productively than a need for money. He had preferred the firm mainly for their flexi-timings. It gave him the luxury of leaving for office well after the rush hour (which in his view was now almost the whole day). He commuted by local train to his office in the city.

As soon as he stepped out from the auto at the station he was accosted by a little girl with an idol on a plate. The idea was two-fold. Most Indians being very religious (more out of fear than reverence) wouldn't mind an offering. Never mind that they would have started their day praying at their shrines at home. And since the auto driver usually returned change in coins, it was convenient to ask for that coin in the passenger's hand. Surprisingly, people did not think much of small change. But before the girl could start, he glared, "Go away before I send you to the God you are asking money for!"

He entered the railway station brushing off the morning's irritation. He looked towards the ticket counters. He had yet to renew his monthly pass. He would have to stand in the queue. It didn't help his mood that one of the ticket windows was closed. The automatic ticket dispensers didn't work. It was frustrating when facilities provided didn't facilitate anything. It would have been better not to have them at all.

The queue at the ticket counter stretched a long way. Each counter was taking its own time. *Population beyond explosion.* He grumbled within himself. *What a country we would have been with half the population! We are not creating a great country. Just a huge labor force for MNCs and a large market for companies.*

Like elements in a formulaic script essential for the story to run, the train station had certain familiar scenarios.

A woman would approach a person standing ahead in the queue. Handing over money for the ticket, she would request the man or woman to buy her ticket as well. The reasons cited would be meant to invoke sympathy, urgency or chivalry.

There would be delays because a commuter at the ticket window would not have tendered the correct amount. This, inspite of instructions written in three languages - Hindi, English and the local language. Uncaringly a Rs. 500 note or mercifully a Rs.100 note would have been handed over for a one way ticket costing only Rs.25. Without fail there would be a fuming or a confused person returning to the counter claiming that the ticket seller had not given the correct amount in change.

And once in a while grumbling in the line would grow louder when someone would go directly to the window without standing in the queue. That he wanted a first class ticket and was thus entitled to direct access was no solace to the majority crowd suffering yet another indignity of being common mass.

Standing in the queue the part time office goer and full time beggar hater saw the familiar family of beggars loitering around. He sighed. His trigger points were everywhere. This family probably had the business rights for this station. *How much of their daily earnings did they have to part with? How much did it cost to get such a lucrative post?*

Each ticket counter had railings to demarcate one queue from another. This forced people to be in a line and not mob the window. At the counter, the railing had an opening to the left for the person to move out. Beggars strategically positioned themselves right next to this opening cashing on the vulnerability of the target. People would have received change for the ticket and so there was ready money to ask for. There was no way of avoiding the beggars who would have already started with their pleas as soon as someone entered the "zone" – their designated area of operation. Kids sometimes would reach out as if to touch. The already disgusted individual would hastily hand over a coin just to avoid the grimy hands.

The man knew that an encounter with a beggar was inevitable. He geared himself for the impending unpleasantness. There was no way out. He had already shooed away an elderly one. He distracted himself by studying the hoardings. Clusters of advertising all around the station competed for the split second attention span of distracted commuters.

It was a while before he reached where the railings began. Not surprisingly the long queue had moved like a snail. Adding to the delay, the counter closed for tea break and would reopen in 15 minutes. The crowd had reduced to a comfortable number. From very crowded it had reduced to just enough to avoid being bumped into. In this city there was no concept of 'sparsely populated'. The routine rush of the daily commuter had ceased. Now it consisted chiefly of families and infrequent travelers.

Those standing between the railings had nowhere to go. Like a car in a one-way street jam, they could move only ahead and only when the window reopened. Knowing this, the beggars took their time with each prospect. They were doubling their pleas, negotiating or asking for food instead. They spent more time than usual on each individual.

The already harried man saw a beggar boy working his way ahead in the line. The boy was around 5 years old with a dirty face and shabby clothes. He seemed new at the station. *Probably sent here for special internship. He must have shown early signs of talent.* His thoughts were getting sarcastic, sharpening the cutting words he would use if needed. He was relieved to see that the boy was not disabled. He could afford to be rude without guilt. He was not a bad man by heart - just disillusioned with the world.

Looking around, he realized that in comparison to the rest of the lot in his queue, he seemed the most affluent. Someone for whom a rupee or two should be negligible. He groaned inwardly as he saw that the boy seemed to draw this exact assumption too. Even while the kid worked his way through the line steadfastly, there were expectant glances in his direction. Eventually, the kid finished with his pleas to an old lady standing before him. He then looked at his 'affluent target' with greater expectations. The 'target' geared up for the assault, already seething at being considered a potential victim.

As the boy approached, the highly alert elderly man looked up at the hoardings again. He studied them intensely. The grand proclamations of gross consumerism shouted - '100% Success' through tuition classes, 'Big Money' through 'work-from-home' schemes, 'Beauty Transformation' by beauty salons, 'Change Destiny' by astrologers. But even these seemed more acceptable than the business of misery and suffering.

"Saheb, kuchch de do na. Ek rupaiyya. Kuchch bhi." "Sir please give something. One rupee. Anything." The boy began his pitch in Hindi. *"Ja. Aage ja. Idhar kucch nahin milega."* "Go away. Move on. Nothing for you here." The man retorted without shifting his gaze from the hoardings. *The Vacuum Cleaner looks so useful. Goes well with the manicured hands of the model.*

"Ab tak kuchch nahin khaya saheb. Meri chhoti behan bhi bhooki hai. Uske liye khana lana hai. Hum dono yahan akele hai." "I've not eaten for the whole day so far, Sir. My little sister is also hungry. She is waiting for me to get her food. We are both alone here."

"Don't give me that dumb stuff. Move on! I don't give money. And I have no food with me. Don't waste your time with me. Go ahead!"

The boy bent down to touch the man's feet. This was one of the common tactics. Give money to avoid getting dirty grimy hands on you or your stuff.

"Don't touch me!" the man shouted in disgust. He glared at the boy to scare him. For a moment, he was struck by the baby face. This really was a fragile little kid. The harshness of the world had not yet become a permanent feature of him. The elderly man spluttered, momentarily caught off balance. His mind and heart were in conflict. Did this one deserve the sting of his reactions?

But the boy had not budged and was on his knees. With folded hands the kid put his head near his potential benefactor's feet. Was this genuine desperation or professional perseverance? The boy whined, "Only one rupee, Sir. You also know it will not get me anything. I am not asking for much. Please Sir."

This was getting too much to bear. The soft spot for the kid was drowning in a sea of anger. Why was this beggar not taking him seriously? Was there something about him that didn't make the boy obey him? Did he look so gullible? People were giving them curious glances adding to his discomfort. They had not been subjected to the extra attention that the boy was now showering on the well-dressed gentleman. The scene unfolding was a welcome distraction from the monotony of standing in a queue.

The ticket counter opened on time and the line started to move. *Small mercy!* The flustered man quickly removed a 20 Rs. note and a 5 Rs. coin for the ticket. As a former banker, he was particular about money He always gave the exact amount. It saved time and avoided hassles.

The sight of money energized the boy. He began pleading vigorously with hand gestures that almost touched the gentleman. *This is too much!* The man swung his hand angrily as if to hit the urchin. Recoiling in fright the boy backed off.

People saw a man in his fifties fuming and waving a beggar away in a wild motion of the hand. The old man's fingers were sweaty in the heat and humidity. In horror he saw the 5 Rs. coin slip out of his hand and bounce on the floor! As if in slow motion it rolled obediently towards the little beggar. With a swirl it lay near his dirty bare feet.

For some reason people get more impatient as they near any counter. All it does is add pressure to the prevalent stressful atmosphere. The queue movement remains the same.

The exasperated elderly man progressed closer towards the ticket window and deeper between the railings. His bitter curses were almost audible. *How could I have been so careless? That bloody kid!* He had made of fool of himself and that too for a beggar. He couldn't get out of the line to retrieve the coin even if he wanted to. He could bring himself to let go of the loss of Rs. 5 (eventually) but not the fact that he had lost the battle with a beggar. For a kid asking for one rupee, five was a bonanza! Now it had saved him the labour of asking money from five others. Whatever amount he would earn that day, this 5 rupee coin was bonus. Of all the people in the damn station the coin had to roll to that kid! No way would he ask the kid to return his coin. Now he wished he had given that miserable boy a rupee. At least the net loss would have been only one rupee.

He stared at the ground to hide his visible anger and embarrassment. *I'm sure people are laughing at me!*

Why the hell did I stand in this line? How I hate these scum! He was lost in thought, still fretting when he heard, "*Saheb! Saheb!*" Turning to his side he saw the little beggar at his feet again. The boy was tugging at his pants with one arm outstretched.

The gentleman citizen reddened with rage. He couldn't control his anger any longer. "*Abhi kya hai kameene?* Now what is it, you rascal!?" he shouted. The sweat, the noise, the crowd, the waiting, the beggar and his own humiliation had finally overpowered him.

The little boy stood up, staring wide in surprise. His innocent eyes suddenly filled with tears. The lips quivered. He was trying hard not to cry. He opened his outstretched fist to reveal the 5 Rs. coin in his palm. "*Aapka paisa. Gir gaya tha.* Your money. It had fallen," he squeaked, barely audible.

The elderly man looked at him, confused. At first he couldn't comprehend what he had just heard. Was this beggar actually offering him his money back? By the rules of the present day selfish world, could the coin be now said to belong to him? It was found on the floor of a public place. It could be anyone's. And this kid was giving it back because he had seen it in his hand? What was making this kid do this? Values? Ethics? Innocence of a kid not yet poisoned by humanity? Honesty? Stupidity born out of ignorance?

"*Tum ne woh paisa kyon nahin liya*? Why did you not take the coin?"

"*Yeh aapka hai na? Aapne diya nahin mujhe . Fir main kaise loon?* "it's yours, no? And you did not give it me. So how can I take it?"

Stunned, the 'world-is-fucked-up-and-I-hate-it' gentleman found himself mechanically taking the money, still watching those teary eyes. He had reached the ticket window by now. He mumbled his destination aware only of the heaviness in his heart. There seemed to be pin drop silence. All he heard was his heart beating. It felt like the thud of a heavy stone pounding grains to powder. He took his ticket without a word and moved on.

At the railway platform he stared at the hoardings. But the slogans appeared as individual words and the pictures just images. There seemed no meaning at all. All his life he had seen cold heartedness, misery and the necessity of being tough in this city. It was the only way to survive. And to do well one had to graduate to a different level of stone heartedness.

What he had witnessed was something very rare. Like seeing the *exact* moment when a caterpillar became a butterfly. Like noticing the tiny micro-moment between breathing in and breathing out when we don't breathe at all. Had he seen a person's dignity beneath the identity of a beggar? Had he seen a rare person with a good heart? Had he been lucky to see the goodness in a person before life's bitterness changed him forever?

The man turned back and walked towards the ticket counters. The little beggar was sitting near the *paan* stained walls taking a break. Making the most of it, his hand was outstretched. The boy cast nervous glances as he saw who was approaching him. What was he going to be subjected to now? He froze as the elderly man came to him and leaned down without a word. Their eyes met. There was apprehension in the little one. The boy pressed against the wall instinctively. As the gentleman walked away silently, the boy looked into his palm in wonder. In it was a 5 Rs. coin.

The Village Couple

We were four friends studying in a college in a rural town. In the '90s an apartment flat was still a new concept in this town that had always preferred traditional row houses. Some city guy must have had the bright idea of converting his plot into flats and making money. It worked. All flats were taken even though the building was not well located. It was surrounded on three sides by shanties of the poor and the fourth side was an open ground.

We wanted independence from hostel life. So we had rented a flat on the third floor of this four storied building. The flat faced sections of the shanty. A major part of the shanty was occupied by a group of south Indian families who had a flourishing business selling *Idlis* and *Dosas* on the footpaths around town. The rest of the shanty was occupied by local labor class. The resident population ranged from the poor to very poor. Unless one was fascinated by their lives there wasn't anything to captivate our interest.

Living so close to a slum aroused curiosity at first. But like everything else it seemed normal after a while.

Some aspects might seem unique to those not exposed to the rural poor. There were broken public toilets or fields to answer the call of nature. But for women, it had to be very early in the morning, almost 4 am onwards to ensure privacy. (You realize this only when you have been up all night cramming for the exams next day.) Then there was the open air bathroom. The wall was made of *sari* or sheets tied around four poles. The top was not covered. No one had expected a high rise to come up. Even after our building came up, no one dared look because the bather always had an eye out for peeping toms.

The houses were small, closely packed on both sides of a small path. An odd cycle, a rare bike or a cow differentiated the 'better of' from the rest. The houses facing our balcony were luckier. The path between their houses and our building boundary had been kept pretty wide for vehicles to pass. Another unspoken reason could have been to keep a respectable distance between the building and the shanty.

The four of us had been close friends for almost two years. Every other day we would sit in the balcony after dinner and yap till late at night.

A few months after we moved in, events occurred that would become unforgettable memories of our college life. We witnessed scenes that were at first disturbing, later interesting and then a routine nuisance. Little did we know that it would end in irreversible outcomes.

Every fortnightly Friday, workers at the local factories got their pay. I'm not sure why it was every alternate week instead of the usual monthly system. Maybe it was to keep them motivated mid-month. Ready money in hand, Fridays became the day for having a good time. The country liquor bars would be fuller than usual. So would the movie halls (especially the obscure mini-theatre showing X-rated movies). The prostitutes at the far end of the town would have had a bigger haul for a night spent.

For college students too fun days depended on availability of money. Hedonistic desires are a great leveler. So Fridays was when they encountered this local crowd more often than not. The melting pot of this diverse crowd was the theatre or the *Paan* shop selling cigarettes. Bars were a different social world altogether. An occasional drunken behavior by the workers or students on a Friday night was expected, though frowned upon.

The Friday antics were nothing to raise eyebrows about. But a man in the shanty below took this to a different level altogether.

He and his wife lived in a house facing our balcony. There was that wide path in front of the house. The couple was the sort that just about made ends meet. The young woman was in her early twenties. She was not beautiful but not unattractive either. The man, in his early thirties, was a labourer in one of the factories. This ordinary couple was no different from others in the shanty.

Except on Fridays.

It was like a well-rehearsed play. Around 10 pm every other Friday the man would come home drunk. On nearing the house he would start shouting. Peppered with abuses to the world in general were abuses to his wife. Staggering towards the house he would drag his wife out. Then the public drama would begin. By now she would be pleading for him to stop and come inside the house. It would anger him further that his wife had the gall to tell him what to do. Over the next half an hour or so, he would mercilessly thrash his wife. Shouting obscenities, he would pull the wailing woman by her hair. She would be showered with brutal kicks and blows. They were not slaps one expected in scuffles between couples.

He seemed to forget he was hitting a woman – his own wife. The violence was vicious. It was as if he was fighting another man and had to win at any cost. Maybe his intention was to hurt and humiliate a woman.

Kicks and blows were specifically targeted at her private parts. He would kick her behind. Hard slaps resounded on buttocks. He would pull her by her breasts. When she lay on the ground weeping and pleading he dragged her by her legs, spreading them apart.

The whole scene was an obscene display of physical and sexual humiliation. The woman would desperately try to hold on to as much dignity as she could manage. At the same time she had to avoid as much physical abuse as possible. The one thing the man didn't do was strip his wife, which wouldn't have been surprising. It seemed he wanted to cause maximum humiliation within his privately defined boundaries.

But he needn't have bothered. His antics stripped the woman in the minds of the viewers. You didn't need to actually see naked breasts or a bare behind when you saw a man getting physical with it. Her *sari* would be in total disarray during the ordeal. There would be enough glimpses of her thighs, midriff and breasts for any voyeur to have got his time's worth. Yes, there were people watching – always. For the humiliation to be public there must be a public.

No one ever said anything. Not that the couple were strangers. They were after all part the same shanty. But it was between husband and wife, wasn't it? Between a man and his woman. Who were they to interfere? And who knows, how many of them did the same in the privacy of their homes. Most of the men secretly enjoyed the show, probably getting aroused for their night sessions.

Within half an hour or so, depending on the demons in the man, the show would end. She would be weeping quietly by then, her energy drained. The soft cries were part exhaustion, part shame and part relief. That part of the evening was done with. He would stumble into the house tired by his manly display. The crowd would disperse with snide remarks and hypocritical laments.

If one lingered after an hour or so there was more to see. The streets were silent. There shone a distant light of a lonely lamppost still functioning. Light from a few flats in the building would reluctantly spread itself, just enough for that house to be seen clearly. By around 11:30 pm, the battered woman would come out to wash utensils outside the house. The *sari* would be just wrapped around herself. Her nakedness underneath was apparent. The thin coarse *sari* failed in its best efforts to provide warmth and privacy. It was obvious that the next sequence of events had been food and sex.

The first time we witnessed the scenes we were shaken. None of us had seen anything like this in real life. We had seen movies and heard of drunken husbands. But to see it live and at such close quarters was unnerving.

The freak show was as fascinating as it was disturbing. We were similar to those people at an accident scene who can't resist seeing the aftermath though they know it will be unpleasant. Like the picture in the newspapers of a man standing on the seashore watching the tsunami wave approach. Logically he should have been running. But its uniqueness fascinated him to a point of folly. Like a twisted joke though we found the brutality of the act disgusting we were also fascinated by the sexuality interspersed in it.

We spent the whole week after that Friday discussing the incident. It was a highlight event of our existence in that town. In the days that followed whenever we saw the woman, all we could think of were the Friday scenes. When the following Friday went uneventful we assumed it had been a one-off occurrence. But over the weeks we realized that there was a pattern to it. Asking around casually we came to know of the fortnightly pay system. This corresponded with the man's behaviour every alternate Fridays. The sequence of events followed a ritual – verbal abuses, beatings, sexually shaded violence, food and sex.

Then an hour later she would be washing utensils in a barely concealing *sari.*

After a few weeks of excitement we got tired of it. That which keeps repeating holds no surprise. It became normal, therefore uninteresting. But disgust and voyeurism was replaced by a sense of helplessness. Each of us had grown up in an environment where domestic abuse was unheard of. For that matter, we hadn't even witnessed street fights. Seeing a woman go through it literally below our noses was bad enough. The harsh reality that it was accepted by the people around made it doubly uncomfortable.

But eventually we got used to the Friday scenes. Even the incentive of watching her in her bare *sari* disappeared after she had glanced up one night towards our balcony. We had no intention of causing embarrassment. So we decided not to sit in the balcony on those Fridays. The windows and the balcony door were kept shut. But our minds couldn't help but turn towards the scenes unfolding below. Occasionally we would glance out to see which phase it had reached. To pass the time, we analysed probable solutions - in theory at least. But there was always that feeling of utter helplessness.

A few months later that changed.

A Bollywood movie called *Krantiveer* was released. It starred Nana Patekar- an actor known for his fiery dialogue delivery and temperamental nature. Scenes from the movie became very popular. Especially rousing speeches made by the actor to take firm action for a good cause. His indomitable screen presence and dialogue delivery made a huge impact on the audience.

We had gone to see the movie at a theatre preferred mainly by the poor. The balcony tickets were cheap. They were readily available because most of that crowd opted for the stalls. The movie made an impact on us too. The quick drinks we had after the movie added to the high. With boosted spirits we set out for the 30 minute walk to our place.

After a while we saw three men ahead on the same road. They seemed drunk. On coming closer it was confirmed they were totally sloshed. One of them looked familiar. Walking past them quickly, we glanced back. The familiar looking guy turned out to be the infamous man in the shanty. Stopping for a cigarette at the fork of a road we watched the men walk past without noticing us. Laughing and shouting at each other they were full of drunken machismo.

Suddenly it struck us. It was that kind of Friday! The night of the public spectacle. The one-woman circus show would commence shortly. She was the whole gamut of animals on display. She was the freak show. She was the joker. She was the joke. Energized by booze the ringmaster was ready to crack the whip.

Where the road forked the two men took a left turn towards the inner part of the town while our man took the one leading to his house. We followed him towards our common destination. The road at that late hour was deserted. The desolate stretch had banyan trees on one side and a field on the other.

We four friends looked at each other. We read each other's minds. Months of anger and helplessness, mixed with alcohol and adrenaline triggered by the movie had become a deadly cocktail.

He was alone, disoriented and drunk. We were four, focused and high. There was no one around. Somehow we all knew what each one was thinking. It was as if providence had set the stage. All we had to do now was act.

As if synchronized by plan, we set to do what was inevitable. The strongest among us ran ahead. He grabbed the staggering man's neck from behind and brought him down. We then dragged the confused heap of a man in the field.

A maneuver popular in the hostel was to cover the victim's face with a bedsheet before beating him or snatching his stuff (usually food brought from home.) It disoriented him. He wouldn't know whom to hit back or what was being done to him. And he wouldn't know who the culprits were.

The man was pinned to the muddy ground. His face was buried in the weeds. There was no one to hear his scared confused shouts. We tore off his shirt and covered his face with it. All of us were breathless but we were careful not to make a sound or utter a word. The urge to hurl abuses was restrained.

The vehemence of our repressed abuses was channeled into kicks and punches. Not a single part of his body was spared. There was not a moment spared. His pajamas were torn away leaving him in his knee length underpants. The money was left alone. We weren't thieves. We knew his economic condition. However we took no pity on his physical condition. One of us couldn't resist burning a spot on each of his buttocks with a cigarette. Smoking was definitely injurious to health! After a quick severe thrashing we left behind a semi- naked man, badly bruised and wailing in pain.

We ran all the way to our apartment in a life affirming thrill never felt before. We were shouting abuses, jumping, fisting the air - the adrenaline still running through. We felt like superheroes avenging the weak in the stillness of the night. Batmen, anyone? We represented the idealistic youth that still believed in societal good. We had set right the injustice cruelly inflicted on a poor helpless woman. And we didn't expect anything in return, did we? We had seen to it that at last the man had paid dearly for his deeds. The woman had finally been rescued from her ordeal.

We ran up to the flat and waited to see what happened next. We dared not sit in the balcony. We doubted we could keep our guilty expressions in check. We were sure he had not seen us but why take a chance? What would happen tonight? Would he vent his frustration with even more savagery or would he realize his folly and treat his wife well?

From a distance we saw the man stagger towards the house. A few cheeky perverts were already present, pretending to have been there just by chance. The woman was inside probably readying herself for the torture. Someone shouted "*Arey*, what happened to you? Shot your limit a bit too much today?" But the laughter was puzzled. For the drunkard to have stumbled in a ditch was expected. But the man was not only dirty but also badly bruised, bare chested, bare foot and in underpants.

Someone called out to his wife. She came out hesitantly. When she saw his condition she gave a loud scream. She approached him warily asking how he got himself in this state, whether he was alright. Still asking questions she led him gently inside. But the man was silent and in a daze. The drunkenness, the beatings and the shock seemed to have numbed him. For once that kind of Friday was a quiet one. For the woman though, the Friday remained the same. Physical agony was replaced by emotional agony at the state of her husband.

We were happy though. Gave each other back slaps. The mission was accomplished. The man would think twice about torturing his wife. He had probably learnt his lesson. The quiet evening was the icing on the cake. We felt a glow of achievement. We had joined the ranks of unsung heroes who had brought a social change. We had earned good karma.

Fortnights following the incident saw no repeat of the scenes of the past. The man had changed after all. The next few weeks passed in hectic college submissions and exams. No time to think about the world nor laze about in the balcony. Soon college ended and we went home for the vacations.

Three weeks later the four of us returned to college for the new semester and resumed our routine. Fridays came and nothing happened. Out of curiosity we sought out the woman. She seemed the same. Her life was as if a series of one struggle after another. What had we expected anyway? Cinderella living her life as a princess? Beauty and the reformed Beast? But we did take heart in the fact that her public ordeal had ended. That itself must have surely given her some solace.

One evening a few weeks later, we met a lady who stayed in our apartment. Her husband owned the hotel which served as our mess. He was away so she was minding it for the time being. She volunteered in a women's welfare center. It also served as an informal community center for women.

Post dinner we sat with her outside the hotel while her people were busy closing up for the day. Small talk here and there finally led to the subject of the couple. "You boys must have had a good time-pass all along," she said with a twinkle in her eye. "That too premium balcony seats," she gave us knowing looks. We sheepishly admitted to it but self-righteously also condemned the man's acts. We lambasted him within limits permitted in presence of an elderly lady.

"Well, it seems he has changed for the better. Now that it has all ended," one of us said. She gave us a long look. "An ending always signals the beginning of something else," she said philosophically. We gave her a blank look. She sighed at the apparent naivety of these young students whose real lessons in life would begin after they left college. We listened in silence as she explained her remark.

"The woman had come to the welfare center a few days after her husband was beaten. She was in total despair. Her visit to the center after her Friday beatings was normal. She would be treated for her bruises and be comforted by the women. Then she would be off to carry on with her life. It was no big deal.

But this time she had the bearings of a person who was lost beyond comprehension. She *had* lost everything but didn't know why. She related to us how that night's incident had crushed her world altogether.

Her husband claimed that it was a revenge attack masterminded by her. According to him, there had to be another man in her life. No one else except a man involved with a woman would do such a thing. It seems the husband had come to this conclusion from his experiences, from movies, and from opinions of the other men he had talked to. As per him there could be no other logical explanation."

The elderly lady paused her narrative to talk to the hotel employees. She asked them to go ahead after they had finished. She would go home in our company. She then continued with the woman's story.

"The poor woman told us that her husband knew that he was a nobody - not worth anyone's time or effort. He had no enemies. He had no close friends. He was just one of the many inconsequential workers at the factory who went about doing his ordinary work for ordinary pay. So who would have a grudge against him and why? The fortnight's pay was still in his pocket so it could not be a robbery attempt. There was ample time to take his money. So her husband believed it could only have been a hate filled act instigated by his wife and her paramour. He even said that the attack was meant to kill him but he survived.

The distraught woman told us that for two days the man had made a ruckus. The suspicions would not go away. All the pleadings and the denials were in vain. This was even more terrible than the physical abuse. He wanted her out of the house. He wanted her to go back to her parents. Her parents themselves were poor so that was no option. Apart from the responsibility of feeding her, there was shame.

Sadly this woman also suffered the humiliation that her man felt for himself. He no longer wanted to see her as it only reminded him of his suspicions and his ordeal. He even threatened to bring in another woman to replace her.

Adding to their woes, the man now had one less set of clothes. Buying a new set would cost money. Till then, she had to make a new set for him from her own *sari*. She had only two *saris*. Now she has to make do with only one. She has only one *sari* to work in, to sleep in, to wash and wear again."

The lady paused for some internal reflection. There was silence among us. No one knew where to look. Finally one of us asked quietly, "So did it get resolved?"

She shrugged, "Depends on how one looks at it. She had come yesterday to talk her heart out."

"Her husband had been beaten and humiliated. And that had shaken the foundations of her life. And she didn't even know why. She had a simple, sheltered life and had not asked for much. She knew her own abilities and place in life. She had always known what kind of man her husband was and accepted it. Her husband was not a dynamic man. He expected the usual duties from his wife and did what he could. Enduring four hours of alcohol and frustration fueled demonic *avatar* gave her two weeks of comfortable daily existence. In her view it was too small a price to pay. Did she approve of the abuse? No. But she had learnt to balance the unfairness of life in manageable bits.

She understood why a man who has not been given any place in life would like to be someone else for at least a few hours. A fortnight's frustration of being a nobody needed an outlet. He wanted to gain some sense of control and superiority. He was a weak man outside the Friday *avatar* and no one doubted it. Including him. But that day's incident had taken away even those few hours from him. And with her life being linked to his both their lives had crumbled.

After a lot of pleadings and intervention from others she has been allowed to stay. That issue is resolved.

113

But there was a heavy price to pay. Her parents had to gift money as a goodwill gesture to appease his hurt feelings. She had known that he occasionally visited prostitutes in secret. But now he is open about it, giving her 'affair' as a ready excuse. She said she will have to wait patiently for him to forget the incident. He will have to show signs that life is back to normal between them. She knows it will take a lot of time. But she is ready to wait because she has no choice."

Looking for some hope one of us asked the elderly lady the obvious question.

"Oh yes," she responded "We also asked the poor wife what would be the sign that all was good between them. With her eyes down she had replied 'The Friday night public drama'."

The Tramp Girl

Rohan and Akash, childhood buddies always bunked the last two lectures at college. The college was lenient about attendance with the misplaced belief that students would make good use of their time. The 'good' use was subject to one's own interpretation. Like most students they didn't stay beyond the stipulated time. Any opportunity to leave early was taken.

Mumbai city owes much of its vibrancy to the local train system – often called the lifeline of the city. It is broadly classified into Western, Central and Harbour Lines. Quite many people's lives revolve around railway stations – the train schedule, the distance for the commute, the crowd in the train (quality-wise, quantity-wise), the time taken and so on.

The college was located in a Mumbai suburb while the two boys stayed in the city right after Mumbai city limits. Hence geographically though separate cities; they were part of the same Central railway line. The evening rush hour in the city began by 4 pm. So they skipped the end of the day lectures to avoid commuter rush. It gave them the luxury of travelling comfortably in the almost empty first class compartment. Unlike the second class compartment one could at least travel in relative comfort in the first class compartment. But the rush hour was a great leveler. Both compartments had equal degrees of discomfort.

For the boys, travelling in the afternoon between 1 pm and 4 pm had perks. They could hang out of the doorway without care and watch the city go by. They got unrestricted view of the pretty girls at stations and in the trains that passed by. They could just laze on the cushioned seats all by themselves. They usually got the compartment almost to themselves save a few businessmen or students probably with similar ideas. At times some tramp would be sitting near the entrance – an unwanted but unavoidable occurrence in this city.

It was one such regular afternoon. They rushed into the compartment and took their favorite seats – ones that faced the passageway. The train sped towards their destination with halts at the stations in between. Rohan and Akash whiled away the time in small talk.

In absence of a new topic the recurring themes were movies, sports and girls.

With unfailing regularity Akash began relating his exploits with his two steady girlfriends. Rohan was never too keen to listen to it. He didn't enjoy his colourful moods. The tales made him green with envy, red with anger at his black luck when it came to girls, finally giving him the blues. After they had exhausted their topics, they drifted to their own worlds, occasionally glancing at passengers.

The train reluctantly stopped at Vidyavihar station which was primarily known for a popular college. A student boarded the train. "Our kind," chuckled Akash. Just as the train began its slow start, a tramp jumped in along with a girl. At once mutterings of annoyance were heard in the background.

Tramps, like beggars were a common sight in the city - irrelevant and invisible. However, in a first class compartment where even the occasional 'non- first-class-looking' type was given unwelcome glances, the tramps were definitely unwelcome. The ample unrestricted space, not available in the second class compartment was a magnet for these tramps. At the most, they would be shooed away with harsh words. But what were such abuses to those abused by fate? But mostly the 'mind-my-own-business' mindset of a big city prevailed. Except for mutterings and scornful looks these tramps were left alone.

The boys were engrossed in their own thoughts and didn't pay attention to the tramps. But they gradually noticed a subtle change in some passengers nearer to the passageway. It is inbuilt in a man's psyche to follow the herd. Today's man is after all, yesterday's primitive animal, dressed up in culture. Anyone staring at the sky will invariably have a few following his gaze. If two men stare at the ground, a crowd will gather around staring at the same place, wondering what the fuss is all about. Finding nothing, they will call the men fools, not realizing their own folly.

Throughout the journey, a man well beyond his middle age had been immersed sternly in 'The Economic Times'. Now, he stared at short intervals at the tramps. In fact his eyes were more frequently gazing ahead than in the newspaper. A man in his 50s with a big paunch, who had been snoring without a care in the world, was staring wide awake at the tramps.

Another commuter beyond the passageway had his back to the tramps. Yet, he could not resist occasional glances behind him. Though all the men maintained a mask of indifference, their furtive gestures exposed their intent. They couldn't resist quick looks despite their demeanor of cultured aloofness.

The two college students were distracted by the sudden buzz of interest. They craned their necks to see what the fuss was all about. The train halted at a signal between Vidyavihar and Ghatkopar stations. One of the tramps got up and walked to the door entrance. The boys looked. With a collective intake of breath they realized what had hooked the men.

A girl tramp was standing in the doorway. She was around 20 years old. Her body was lean and fleshy in the right places - thick thighs, full breasts. Her voluptuous body was open to an eager audience, though not intentionally. She had a surprisingly healthy body for someone with no means of a healthy lifestyle. Her filthy dress was tattered at enough places to expose her to the world. One shoulder was bare while the other was held together by coarse threads. Slits on both sides of her knee length gown reached way above the thighs. It revealed a lot of her long legs. The same kind of dress worn by a celebrity would have been a fashion statement.

But it was not just the carelessly attired body that had captured the attention of the dignified crowd. Show of skin in the media had become a common affair. It influenced the impressionable who believed that to show a lot was a show of individuality. Now it would take a lot more than that for the public to be shocked. What had drawn the reluctant voyeurs beyond the obvious skin show were her looks.

She was one of the most beautiful girls they had ever seen. And probably the only beautiful dirty girl. Her face was a mask of sticky muck. Her head was a mess of wiry unkempt hair. But her eyes! They were perfectly placed in a perfectly featured face. The eyes were bluish green. It was unnatural for a tramp to possess what belonged to an elite woman - eyes associated with beauty and status. They spoke a language of their own expounding their uniqueness. When she looked, it was as if the air gave way. Her gaze was pure and devoid of impurity. Only 'she-who-looked' and 'one-looked-at' existed at that moment in time. It cut through resistance and perception, burying itself in the victim's mind or heart, whichever gave in first.

Akash stared, his mouth slightly open. Never before had a girl made such an instant impact. It was usually he who charmed the females. The stud was speechless for once. He was relieved no one had noticed. Self-consciously he looked away. He nudged Rohan's hand only to find Rohan himself in a trance.

The girl seemed oblivious to the effect she was having on the men around. She was probably used to this kind of treatment and worse. Lost in her own world, she paced aimlessly across the passage. She seemed unfazed by the non-verbal, non-physical buzz emanating in the compartment. A gush of air passed through the slits in her dress showcasing even more of what was already being ogled at. But she wasn't bothered by it. She picked her nose vigorously, rolling the mucus and sticking it on the steel handle of the cushioned seat. The audience stared as she scratched her buttocks with her dirty nails, cleared her throat loudly, spat out of the train and returned to her man. The man was stereotype tramp - dirty, unshaven, and unkempt. He was not old enough to be her father but considering the savage life of the street dweller, he could have fathered the girl.

At Kanjurmarg station the tramps got off and disappeared from sight. The train resumed the last 15 minutes of its run. Suddenly there were enough topics to keep Akash and Rohan busy chatting. They decided to nickname her BGs, referring to the bluish green eyes. The name was derived from a '70s pop group, who though popular; no one openly admitted listening to because they sang with an odd high pitched voice.

"Is it possible for ugly to produce beauty?" pondered Rohan. "Must be one of the freaks of fate. 'Lotus– grows-in-the-mud' kinda thing," he answered himself philosophically. "Biology is not just based on economic and social conditions," countered Akash. "Haven't you seen average parents with good looking children and good looking parents having kids with no resemblance? You've heard comments made, right?

You know, when a fair kid is born to dark skinned parents."

The boys reasoned that since the universe had polar opposites to maintain equilibrium, BGs' ugly life circumstances had been compensated with physically enchanting features.

The next day, as usual, the boys left college early and caught the same train - a common habit among daily commuters. Akash and Rohan stood at the doorway of the empty compartment; letting wind brush them as the train sped towards home. The train arrived at Vidyavihar station with the platform on the other side of the doorway. The boys were engrossed checking out the crowd on the station platforms when a strong stench filled the air. They turned towards the nauseating smell and found themselves staring at those bewitching eyes. The tramp girl and her man had entered the compartment. Holding their breath the boys rushed to grab seats which would give them full view of BGs.

Both the boys blushed involuntarily when her eyes stared at them. But there were no signs of any emotion. She gazed past them and covered the rest of the crowd. The boys watched with amusement at the effect on men who were seeing her for the first time. The raw haggard intensity of the gutter woman's presence had more power than the superficial make-up assisted glitter. But unaware of it all, the 'Gutteress' of beauty graced the passage, scratching her dirty mesh of hair.

A man walked to the door to get off at the next stop. Though standing at the other end of the doorway he held a handkerchief to his mouth, not wanting to breathe. Yet as he alighted he could not resist a glance at her.The dirty beauty sat crouched beside her man who had his head between his knees. At the next station they silently got off.

The boys eagerly waited for the three days of the week when they sneaked off early to catch the afternoon train. Their latest excitement was double packed. The suspense of whether BGs would enter their compartment and of watching her when she did. So far the girl and her companion had chosen the same compartment. Having only three days as visible proof, the boys wondered whether the tramps travelled in other trains or in different compartments of the same train. They speculated on the movements of the tramps. The couple boarded at Vidyavihar and got off at Kanjurmarg, which was 10 minutes by train. Was one their home and the other their area of activity? Which was which? That they were beggars or scavengers there was no doubt. But why did they travel by train instead of walking? Was it insolence of travelling in the comfort of a men's first class compartment? Was the young girl a bait to prevent the men from throwing them out?

The boys marveled at the utter lack of reaction in the girl to the constant stares. Life had definitely made her thick skinned. To be oblivious to the emotions she generated was quite a feat. Surely deep inside she had to have ingrained characteristics of every human. Certain factory settings could not be changed. They existed as reminders of man's fallibility.

Physical attractiveness is an important aspect of one's personality. Everyone is sensitive about it. The plain magnify their appealing traits hoping only that would be noticed. Praise people for their intelligence and they will like it. Some might even believe that they deserved it anyways. But praise them for their 'good looks' and they will love it! Believing it to be always true they will admire the flatterer's intelligence in noticing it.

The tramp girl with her enchanting face and a body to match would definitely be conscious of it, regardless of who she was. To maintain such a callous neglect was difficult to fathom. Her clean version would be a sell out in the market of lust. Morality issues chiefly arise in those who have the luxury to contemplate it. Between the stomach and the soul, it is the soul that takes a backseat. Why did she then undervalue it so much?

Such grave intellectual matters kept the boys occupied in their commute. Their journey became a heady mix of anticipation before Vidyavihar station, fascination till Kanjurmarg station and discussion till their destination.

Within six months they were through with college and afternoon trains. Eventually the girl and her blue-green eyes faded from their talks and short term memory.

A few months later the two friends were on their way to a party. Akash was driving his new car. They halted at a traffic signal at a major junction in Kanjurmarg. From there they had to take the road towards Powai.

The guys were excited about the night ahead. Which restaurant to go to? Which new expensive drink to experiment with? (The party was sponsored by their friend) What time to come back home sober enough?

The cacophony of the vehicles interspersed with background noise of the overcrowded city. The boys chatter added to it. The car windows at the front were open for the cool evening breeze.

"*Ek rupaiyya de na*. Give one rupee, no." A very hoarse sound smashed into the interior of the car. The grating voice had a feminine twang but a masculine tone.

Rohan who had his back to the window jumped in surprise and turned to look. Akash had no need to turn. He was staring at the open window behind Rohan.

A familiar sensation drenched them like a bucket of cold water. It was a blast from the past. They were staring into bluish green eyes! It was BGs at close quarters. She was leaning inside the car. The tramp was in her professional role of a beggar. But there were no pleas in her expression or her stance. The asking for alms had been a statement. A seasoned beggar spends not more than a few seconds on an unresponsive target, especially at a traffic signal. There is only so much time to cover the stranded commuters. Seeing no inclination from the two she snorted, leaned back from the window and moved on. She left behind two speechless guys and a lot of stink in the car. Akash hastily closed the windows and switched on the AC. The boys vigorously swished deodorants on themselves and in the car. But as her stench died her memories came to life.

"So this is where they operate," surmised Rohan with approval. "It does have potential. Imagine how many vehicles pass by. So they must be staying in Vidyavihar. That's the station they would board from, no?"

"No," countered Akash, the 'out-of-the-box thinker'. "You've got it wrong. It's the other way round. They operate in Vidyavihar. They spend their day there.

They return to their base somewhere near here. The begging in the evening is just for extras." He started to drive towards the uphill Powai road.

"How can you be so sure?" demanded Rohan. He wanted to win at least a few arguments with Akash.

"You always think the obvious Rohan," said Akash as if talking to a child. "Will someone travel all the way here just to beg only in the evening? Obviously not! Isn't the major part of the day usually spent where you work? Those tramps always returned to Kanjurmarg around 4-5 in the evening. So this must be their area of residence." The 'area of residence' was said with mock sophistication. The discussion trailed off as they neared their rendezvous point.

The party ended at 3 AM, way beyond agreed time. It had continued unexpectedly at another friend's house whose parents were away. By around 4:30 AM Akash and Rohan were in Powai again. The empty roads at dawn would get them home by around 5 AM. But that would not do. They were allowed to stay out late under a tacit understanding between them and their parents. They were to return home either before 11

PM or after 6:30 AM. Partying could not be at the cost of their parents' sleep.

Since there was still time for their conditional arrival at home, they parked the car near Powai Lake. This popular landmark, was surrounded by thick undergrowth. Streetlights and benches were installed around the entrance to the lake. Giving in to the fatigue of the night, the guys pushed back the seats and drifted to sleep.

Akash woke up with a start. A sudden wave of fear filled him as he tried to make sense of his surroundings. As his droopiness receded it became clear why he was in the car facing a lake. He saw Rohan curled uncomfortably in the back seat. Akash was amused at Rohan's relocation to the luxury of the back seat. Rohan was not much of a sleeper. The inert body was the effect of booze. He called out, "Come on Rohan. Get up. Enough sleeping, *yaar*. We have to go." No response.

"Hey Ritu, look at Rohan!" Akash shouted. With a sudden jolt, Rohan sat up in embarrassment. Ritu had once witnessed Rohan's awkward style of sleeping with his hands between his legs. She had cruelly spread a twisted version around as a harmless joke. Since then it had made the ultra-sensitive Rohan extremely conscious of sleeping in public - especially around females.

Seeing no one, he cursed Akash and got out of the car to stretch himself. He watched groggily as the sun moved stealthily to its position of light and might. The golden soothing sky was just a prelude to the blazing heat of the day ahead. He was lost in the beauty of the scene, rarely seen by those who slept through dawn. Black silhouettes were painted colours by the emerging rays. The water in the lake shimmered as the sun appeared to rise from it.

In the silent darkness of the dawn, lives resumed their humdrum existence, unnoticed by the dozing apartments. Slum dwellers used the lake for washing clothes and themselves. An occasional truck driver having spent the night there got ready to move on. The early birds stirred. An orchestra of birdsong began their notes.

Rohan looked around with pleasant curiosity. To be at such a place at such a time was a unique affair for him. His gaze settled upon a figure walking towards the dirtier side of the lake, near a cluster of wild bushes. The walk held his attention. That it was a female, he was sure. He had meant to give a cursory glance but for some reason he was unable to look away. He realized with a shock why he was gazing so intently at the figure. It was the tramp girl - their BGs! Her body had transfixed him too many times for his subconscious to miss the connection. What was she doing here?

He had involuntarily walked ahead in the direction of the figure. Now wide awake, he rushed back to the car. Akash was in the mood to leave as fast as possible. Youngsters out in an expensive car at dawn were vulnerable targets. He frowned as he saw Rohan come to his side of the car. Before he could speak Rohan put a hand on his shoulder. He was in an excited state. He gasped, "Akash! Guess what?"

"What? Get in the car. Fast. We'll talk in the car. Let's go before anyone notices us."

"No! Listen!" He hissed loudly. "I saw her! There! She is there…. Near the lake.

"Who is there? What's wrong with you, man? Let's first get out of here. Then you can tell me whatever."

"The girl! She…is ….there……!"

"Which girl? Rohan! Stop acting crazy," snapped Akash.

"That girl with the bluish green eyes. BGs, remember?

"Nice try Rohan. Ok! Sorry for waking you up with Ritu's name. Now just chill *yaar*! You know we have to reach home fast. I owe you one for my silly prank, ok? Now get in!"

"No! Screw your prank. I didn't even think about it. It's the tramp girl from the train…believe me! Damn you Akash! Just listen! I saw her walking towards the lake. Not this side. We can't see it from here. Towards the right. Just park the car near that point. It's got a lot of wild bushes.Trust me, man. It will take only 2 minutes. We can have a quick look. This is so weird! Let's not lose this chance to discover their mystery location. We've been wondering about it for so long!" Rohan finally took a deep breath.

Seeing Rohan's state Akash relented. Now he too was curious. He edged his car towards the far end of the lake nearer to the bushes. The danger of muggers was relegated down the priority list. They had a target of their own now.

"What is she doing out in the lake?" Akash wondered aloud.

"Call of nature," answered Rohan.

"No way. Not in the open."

"Sleepwalking."

"Come on, Rohan. Seriously."

"Maybe she is connected to the underworld," persisted Rohan.

"Fucking dramatic."

"I wasn't aware there's a qualifying personality for it," retorted Rohan defensively. But he knew his assumption had been silly.

"Let's find out," said Akash with a sense of purpose.

They walked cautiously towards the steps leading to the lake. The steps were dirty. Weeds grew along its edges. This part of the lake was seldom used and therefore neglected. They crouched low trying to be as invisible as possible. They could be seen if anyone looked. But it was better than strutting out in the open. The top step had lampposts on each side, like gateposts, fixed on large concrete blocks. The boys knelt on either side behind the lamp posts. With a clear view of the lake they watched with bated breathe. The scene ahead left them stunned. Time stood still. Everything else faded into nothingness.

The girl had stripped off her filthy gown and wrapped herself in a thin cloth. The transparent cloth had been stretched to the limits of its capability. The cloth reluctantly gave allowance to the fullness of the breasts that it covered. But they in turn fought to express themselves, revealing the tops of the heavy bosom. The deep cleavage could squeeze out all the lust of the observer. The stretched cloth was just enough to cover her privates, leaving her fleshy thunder thighs open to the caress of the wind. She had been standing facing the steps to lay down the gown. As usual she was lost in her own world. She turned towards the water, giving her round, firm buttocks the attention it deserved. The wet cloth clasped protectively at the body, not willing to share the treasure it held within itself.

Treading into the shallow water near the steps, the girl took a big breathe and dipped herself fully in it. The water enveloped her completely. The surrounding area turned dark with grime. The dark patch expanded as the girl emerged. Standing in the water she started scrubbing and washing herself. She was like the Russian matryoshka dolls where larger dolls revealed smaller ones inside. With every wash, layers of dirt peeled away to showcase cleaner shades of BGs.

The tramp girl gradually transformed into a beautiful maiden. It was not beauty by comparison - the dirty becoming clean. What emerged was her original self, hidden by the dirty exterior. The light brown skin reflected a rough life. Jet black hair danced on her shoulders with every movement. Her eyes - those bluish green gems, were full of life. They seemed to glow in secret pleasure.

The boys' wonder was beyond anything experienced before. The lust of seeing a naked female had passed. In its place was awe of an exquisite beauty. The nudes painted by truly great artists transcend their nakedness. The viewer is mesmerized by the aura of the painting as a whole. So stood before them, a living work of art.

The bath finished, the wet girl gathered her gown and started walking up the steps. The young voyeurs were suddenly terrified. Boys from well-brought-up, well-do-to families didn't peek at lowly street girls, did they? What if she screamed for her people? To get into trouble because of a petty beggar would not be good for their well-being – body and ego. They glanced at each other nervously, unsure of what to do. Fortunately she was engrossed with the torn gown in her customary state of trance. She walked past without change in pace or demeanor.

Akash and Rohan couldn't shake off the effect of what they had witnessed. Forgotten was the car, the deadline and the need to get home. Their curiosity was heightened and they wanted to see where it would lead. Now that they knew what she was, they wanted to know who she was.

They decided to follow her from a safe distance. They would stop when she reached her dwelling or her people. At the slightest indication of trouble, they would run for it.

The girl walked deeper into the trees and unkempt vegetation. The boys wondered if her lot lived in the swampy area near the lake. It was possible, though hard to comprehend. The ground softened under their feet as they ventured further into the thick growth.

Rohan's attention was on the mud under his feet. Suddenly Akash stopped him with a hand on his shoulder. There was a crude clearing ahead. It appeared man-made by the careful disruption of its vegetation. They hunched down in front of some bushes outlining the clearing. They didn't bother about the mud. Cautiously they peeked through the partings in the shrubs.

The girl stood naked on the small patch of ground that had been cleared. The wet cloth now off her body was squeezed dry and placed on a bush. The stark naked girl lay on the ground and closed her eyes. She was oblivious to the hypnotizing effect on her secret audience. After a while she got up and reached purposefully into the bushes. Something hidden in them was now in her hand. She sat and began admiring the object. It took a few seconds for the boys to realize what she was doing. They were amazed to see that the object was a broken piece of mirror! She was admiring herself in it! There was a serene smile on her face. She liked what she saw. She caressed the image with her eyes like water spraying a beautiful rose. The moment was an ironic kaleidoscope of emotions. The beggar was being sensitive to beauty. The tramp's vanity befitted a princess.

Images from past and present formed a collage of confusion in the boys. Their muddled emotions added a framework to this picture of doubt. All those times they had watched her they had been wrong. She was neither ignorant of herself nor unaware of her impact on others. She was like most females and quite a few males too. This savage had a civilized soul. Without make-up she was far more beautiful than the average woman in the city. Even the pretty ones needed cosmetics to feel confident of their beauty. And she must be aware of it. Did she then scoff at women when she begged them for alms? Or did the cruelty of life strike her every time she looked at their faces? Judging by her public stance, it must be the scoffing.

Their minds were in a frenzy of thoughts. They were too stunned too move. Had something happened in recent months to turn her into a new leaf? Had she finally decided to capitalize on her physical assets? Had the self-realisation of what she possessed been recent? What had brought about the awareness? Was it an external desire for appreciation or an internal awakening of self- esteem?

After about 10 minutes or so, she stood up, stretched and yawned. She scratched her hair and arms absentmindedly, cleared her throat loudly and spat on the ground. Some things had not changed. Her body had dried. The bluish green eyes looked refreshed. She then took a few steps and knelt near a small ditch of blackish mud. The boys leaned forward in anticipation.

They watch in disbelief as the girl dipped her hands completely into the ditch. Then, taking large clumps of the black sticky mud she splattered it across her full breasts. The excess slimy muck slithered down her stomach and disappeared in her crotch. She repeated the motion several times across her body. Eventually, every part of her naked body was covered in a layer of stinking filth.

The boys recoiled in shock ! They were filled with horror and disgust. The supposedly erotic scene failed to excite the voyeurs. If that mud was replaced with chocolate syrup it would have been a treat. But stinking dirt? The sight was so nauseating that Rohan clamped his nose and mouth. He didn't want to throw up the night's party. But the bizarre scene held them captive. They were rooted to the spot. They looked on uneasily at what she would do next. Having experienced so much in so less a time they needed to see the end of this weird behaviour.

Her face was clean and the stark contrast was scary. Then they saw her bring her cupped palms full of the filth to her face. They could not take it anymore! It was the last straw. They ran back in disgust. It was not worth the discomfort they felt. Curiosity kills a cat and with that it's past and future as well. The price of their curiosity was to live forever with the disgusting memory of her actions. They would never again remember her with the same excitement as before. Given a choice they would not want to remember her at all! Was she crazy? She was definitely not normal. To have beauty was a boon. To feel vain about it was natural too. But to tarnish it in such a disgusting manner was unimaginable. Why then bother with the cleansing ritual?

They were in the car desperate to get away. This was not what they had expected at all. There had been no indication that it would lead to a disgusting finale. They sat silently for a while to catch their breath and clear their thoughts.

Akash's familiar logical side finally took control and he calmed down.

"Let's try to understand why she does it," he began. "Obviously, she has looks that would fit in the best of social circles. But it's a major drawback for someone who has to feed off people's sympathy and superiority complex. No one would give her money in her clean avatar. The dirty profile suits her profession and life. Maybe that's why the fancy dress. Or shall we say fancy mess?" He gave a short scornful laugh which summed up his reaction to the whole drama.

Rohan, the more sensitive of the two, needed more time to get over it. Negative images and feelings rule stronger and often overshadow the positive ones. The mind now contained images of her gorgeously naked clean body. But it chose to project the filthy version and the recollection of the stink. Rohan was having a hard time diverting his mind to pleasant thoughts.

Unable to take it any longer he screamed putting his head out of the window. "Yuck! "For all her looks, and that body of hers I would never touch that stinking, filthy disgusting thing. Not even for a million bucks. Forget touching her man....! Who would even want to go near her?"

The sun shone brightly. As if it knew and was grinning at their ignorance. Silence seemed to fill the car. The boys stared mindlessly at the lake ahead now fully bathed in daylight.

All of a sudden, they turned to one another as if reading each other's mind. Rohan's remark had sparked memories. They both recollected when men in the train would gaze at her with wanton lust from far. But as they neared her to alight at their station, they would gag at the stench. They would close their mouths and nose in automatic disgust. Their whole being would say NO to the girl with bluish green eyes who had been so desirable from a distance.

So that was it! They stared at each other as if enlightened. Was this the real answer? Man had thousand reservations to a thousand issues. The endless list had universally common ones. Looks, color of skin, nationality, religion, community, place of origin, money, veg, non-veg to name a few. But woman as a sex object transcended even the most rigid. It broke barriers of religion, age, class and even looks for a desperate man. What chance then did a vulnerable, unprotected street dweller have? And with beauty like hers, it was a curse compounded many times over.

Civilized she might not be, but the girl had developed her own set of rules in the jungle of life. Maybe her personal dignity was the only real value she possessed. And she was trying to hold on to it as much as she could. In a peculiar twist of principle she was ready to sell her respect in the eyes of the world but not her body. She would endure harsh looks, words and even bear the stench as her faithful companion, just to deny anyone what they would have given anything for. She was like that diamond buried deep underground in the mines. To possess it one had to dig deep into the dirt and become a part of the dirty process. But man, by proclaiming himself to be the highest form of life revealed his lowest stature. She must have realised that man was shallow, just like the society he had created. Only skin deep.

After thorough contemplation Akash and Rohan concluded that their reasoning could be the only truth. They didn't need proof or validation from her. They just knew it. Those bluish green eyes lead to an intelligent soul deep inside the abyss. The gutter had its virtues too. Just that no one ventured into it in search of misplaced treasures. The label 'gutter' stopped them.

The girl tramp emerged from the undergrowth. It was time to get into her public persona. Her eyes sparkled in the morning sun. They turned to watch her. Her eyes met their gaze in turn.

The respect for her was apparent on their faces. She must have sensed it too, for this time there was no look of stony ignorance.

With a knowing smile, she gave them a smirk of acknowledgement and walked away.

The Borrower

"How the kids have grown," observed the elderly man affectionately as he looked out of his 3rd floor balcony. "It seems just yesterday that these kids were trudging off to school in their teeny weeny uniforms," he added. "Well, for some of these girls it's still yesterday," responded his wife sarcastically as she cut vegetables for dinner. "They have forgotten that they have grown. Their dresses are still teeny weeny. Probably the same ones from their childhood." His wife, the 'no-nonsense' type, always spoke her mind.

The graceful couple, in their late sixties lived in a far off suburb of a cosmopolitan city. Though far enough from the heart of the city, it was within the municipal limits. Their address and thus their identity was intrinsically linked with it. The now old man had settled in this unsought suburb almost 40 years ago, when it was sparsely populated. As a young bachelor this was what he could afford with his savings and borrowings. The joy of owning a house in "The City" had compensated for the lack of infrastructure in this once nascent distant suburb. In the early years it had been a difficult commute to work and they had to make do with fewer facilities. As with every popular place, the area developed. So did demand for homes for the steady flow of hopefuls. He had aged watching the gradual transformation of his area. From a swampy land of trees and muddy roads it became a well-planned locality. Initially it was made up of simple middle class. The majority population now consisted of the upper middle class and the rich staying in classy apartments. He could safely boast that his suburb was one of the rare places where it was hard to find visible slums. Sure, there were shanties of the poor but they were secluded. Over the years, posh restaurants, expensive shops and focal point of local buses added to the status of the place.

Every evening he would take a walk near his house. Except for the ill-maintained road, changes came about every few years. Like a monthly calendar that needed to be changed periodically to avoid becoming irrelevant, the surrounding landscape kept redefining itself. Shops sprouted on empty lands. Posh buildings replaced abandoned waste land. Certain advancements baffled him - like the AC Hair Cutting Saloon? *Why did one need an air-conditioned saloon to get a haircut?* ACs had been associated with luxury. There was a time when AC vents protruding from the walls of the buildings proclaimed the high status of its residents.

Faithful to its roots and its past the Gulmohar trees along the street remained unchanged. Indifferent to the changes around, it bloomed with a grace unlike the man-made structures. He always felt a warm glow seeing the trees. Many years ago, he had been one of the crusaders of the tree plantation movement. The idea had been to add beauty to the surroundings while providing a leafy shade for pedestrians. This had not gone well with some affluent residents whose elegant buildings and therefore, their status would get hidden. The vocalized reason was that they could no longer view the streets and that trees would attract birds that would dirty their balconies. Fortunately the mindset in those days leaned towards 'state-of-majority-of-us' than status. The Gulmohars reigned supreme.

With the changing landscape, the elderly gentleman noticed the changing attitudes of people. Bonds became indicators of aspirations and status. The "who" you knew depended on the "why". The current world even had a socially accepted word for it – 'Networking'. That a friend was essentially a part of a network said something about the prevalent society.

The shift from middle age to old age became more obvious watching kids in the locality grow up into adults. The transition from innocence to worldliness with scope for world-weariness spared no one. It was not just the physical aspect that redefined them. The emotional, social and behavioral changes spoke louder than looks.

This awareness heightened when he encountered them. Like the pig tailed little girl who used to chirp a "Hello Uncle" through her school years now barely looked up when she passed by. She had grown into a petite woman in her twenties. *Was it the weight of the world? Was there a norm on how matured young woman should behave in public? Was it uncool to be seen talking with old folks?*

Then there was the 'What do you want to be when you grow up?' asked ritually to kids in India. No matter that most adults had not found the answer themselves. Having seen these youngsters as toddlers, it was interesting to note how many of them had lived up to expectations and how many had fallen short. There were surprises as always. Not that any of this affected his life. These musings were just 'thought entertainment'.

He took the familiar turn of the road. There were the usual group of guys. Every evening, like birds flocking to their favourite tree, they assembled at the corner *paan* shop. The circus of youth would be on display. Cigarette in hand, music blaring from one car, they checked out the passing crowd. When they saw him the cigarette was hidden or flicked away depending on how much of it was left. He smiled at their gesture of respect and they acknowledged it in turn.

These guys were in their thirties. Each ran a family business. *How strange life was.* He mused as he waved back at them and walked on. They would have topped the "least likely to succeed" list. Right from childhood they were stereotypes of rich spoilt brats. Their only focus had been a hedonistic life which had welcomed them with a red carpet. They had graduated to smoking, drinking and numerous affairs (too many to remain a secret). As age caught up, (or maturity) they had cooled down considerably. Not much was heard about them in public gossip. Now they were seen only in the evenings.

The elderly man lived with the times and accepted the changing mindset of the younger generation. He wisely knew what he could change and what he had to get used to. Moreover, his ability to see other's point of view had made him a popular counselor and confidant.

He was always ready to guide and lend a patient ear to anyone seeking it. Having come from a small town his only abundance had been ignorance and naivety. Though missing opportunities along the way he had managed to raise his stature to that of a relatively successful middle class retiree. But he knew that had he received guidance and support he would have been much more successful than what he had finally achieved. From this regret arose his passion for helping people. He prided himself in being unlike those who grumbled about the present, harped about the better days of the past but didn't participate to make a difference.

One day, late afternoon the doorbell of his flat rang. He had just woken from his siesta. Lazily he sauntered towards the door. "Uncle may I come in", stuttered the visitor, Kumar. Kumar had a few days' stubble and looked weary. It was unclear whether his eyes were red from fatigue or alcohol.

"Of course, Kumar. Please come in," invited the old man. He led Kumar to the living room sofa and sat on the chair across him. Kumar had a look of uncertainty and hesitation. There was something amiss.

"So? How's life? How is business? This is a good season for your work, no?"

There was no response. The shabby young man was lost in some private dialogue. He was preparing himself to explain his visit.

To fill in the silence the old man joked, "It is time to find a suitable wife for you. You are one of the most eligible bachelors in our area." *This man needs to relax.*

Kumar gave a weak smile. His hands were fidgety. He was restless. He was keen to get to the point. This was no social visit.

"Uncle," he began, "I need help". The uncle nodded knowingly. He patiently waited for Kumar to continue. The old man's instinct had been right about the situation. He readied himself to take on the role of a counselor.

"Uncle, I am in trouble".

"What sort of trouble?"

"I made some bad investments and business has collapsed. To recover the losses I rashly played the stock market and lost money there too. I need to repay the debts. I need help. I'm ready for any job. Anything to get money flowing in."

"I'm sorry to hear this Kumar. Don't worry. I will be on the lookout for any jobs suited for you. I will ask around. Most of my friends are retired so it might take a while. But I will surely work on it."

"It's not that kind of help I am asking for, Uncle" replied Kumar awkwardly. "I desperately need Rs.2000. I promise to return it as soon as possible."

"But where can I…?"

"Please Uncle! I have come with great hopes. I am going through hell. Otherwise I wouldn't have come to you like this".

The old man was silent. His idealistic philosophy was debating with his worldly-wise side. His idea of help had always been the non-financial type. He believed that giving one's time and shoulder to cry on was in itself precious in today's self-centered world. He was not a rich man to give away money. (How many of the rich did?) In today's world Rs.2000 might sound trivial. He knew kids didn't hesitate to spend that kind of money in a day. But for him that was a big amount to contend with. In some aspects he was still tuned to the era when 'paise' had value and Rs.100 got you more than a little something. Rs.2000 was not a small amount for a retired man like him. And what if it started a precedent? How could he say no to the next one who came asking for money- no matter the amount?

He asked Kumar to wait while he checked whether he had the money. He walked to the bedroom unsure of his decision. Impractical though it was, he had never shied away from helping anyone. And this was the first time someone from a well-off family had approached him for money. He convinced himself that it was a genuine need. (Thank God his wife was away visiting her sister). He took the money from the cupboard and handed it over to Kumar.

"Thank you Uncle!" Kumar said earnestly. "I will return the money as soon as possible. You have been a great help. Thank you very much."

Closing the door the old man sat on the sofa. His mind was restless. The unexpected loss of money and Kumar's state disturbed him. Kumar hailed from a rich family. His circle of friends was the group the old man encountered every evening. These guys represented the 'good – fated' types.They would be always assumed to lead smooth lives. Their downs would still be higher than the average person's average phase. Picture a billionaire who is down on his luck. He loses a few millions, is out of the top richest list but is still a very rich man.

Kumar begging around for petty money was strange and out of character. Moreover the kind old man was just one of the friendly uncles in the neighborhood. He was not a family friend nor was he close to these guys. Advice had been always free. All it took was his retirement hours. To be approached for a delicate issue like money was a different matter altogether. *Am I a last resort?* Or worse. *Am I been taken advantage of?*

The day ahead bore bitter fruits of his generosity. He had been scolded by his wife the rest of the day. "Why did he not go to one of his rich friends? That amount is peanuts to them. Have you forgotten that every rupee is important to us in our old age? Or have you started a money lending business now? 'Heart of gold' seems to have been taken quite literally." Such valid comments laced with her customary sarcasm pricked. It was pointless trying to defend himself because she was right.

The next day the solemn gentleman set out for his evening walk. Thank heavens for this routine! It gave him an excuse to stay away from his wife for a few hours. Had she been wrong he would have argued. But he realized his mistake. Nothing could be done about it now.

He encountered the usual group again. "Hello Uncle," they chorused.

"Time pass?" he asked, smiling.

"What to do Uncle? We get only this time to relax," replied one of them.

"Where is your friend Kumar? What's with him nowadays?"

"Why, Uncle?" someone asked. The group became a little wary. Their body language less casual.

The old man then frankly related the previous afternoon's incident. He had pondered about this on the way. Maybe Kumar's friends could shed some light. If it was bad, he would be forewarned.

The group looked at each other. Each was waiting for the other to speak. Finally, one timid sort of guy said, "Be careful of Kumar, Uncle. We have stopped keeping in touch with him. He has lost his way."

"Lost his way is so diplomatic, *yaar*," an outspoken member of the group joined in. "Uncle, we are very free with you. So let me be frank. You know that we all drink, smoke, party hard. That's no secret. But even we have limits. We have to go home to our families and you know how that is. But lately Kumar has gone overboard. He is constantly in need of money. We don't know what kind of trouble he is in. But obviously it's not the right kind."

"As if there is a right and wrong kind," commented someone else casually, adding his two cents to the conversation.

"Yes there is," insisted the outspoken person. "The right kind is the one that can be discussed with family and friends. That can be dealt with openly. The wrong kind is everything else. Uncle, you know that we are all in business. There are days of losses and there are days of profit. So we are comfortable with lending and borrowing. But nowadays Kumar keeps asking money from whoever he can approach. I think by now he must have run out of people. Stay away from him for a while. Refuse to give money if he comes again. You don't have to feel bad about it."

That night the 'do-gooder' had trouble sleeping. The evening's conversation had shaken him. His restless mind kept reflecting on the issue. Moral decline of the society, a distant entity till then, had reached his doorsteps. It had made him a target too. So far such incidents had been only news or someone else's problem. That it had actually happened to him was difficult to comprehend. All the advice (*'gyaan'*) he gave to others seemed to elude him. He was unable to resolve it in his mind.

Kumar had been given a 'thumbs-down' by his own friends. That they too had refused to help him said a lot about Kumar's situation. This was yet another prevalent version of friendship. But what hurt the old man was that only *he* seemed to have been foolish. Kumar had found a channel for his needs. The old man's final thought before drifting to an uneasy sleep was to avoid his borrower at all costs.

A few days later the elderly citizen set out for the regular trip to the market. He preferred walking. But with the passing years it had become less enjoyable - what with the increasing crowd and the hawkers. Within half an hour, the shopping done, he set out for the 15 minute walk back home. The elderly couple's needs being minimal the bags were never heavy. It saved him the hassle of getting an auto. Anyways he didn't approve of the fare which in his opinion was pretty high for such a short distance.

"Uncle!" someone called from behind. The elderly man didn't look back. He was busy negotiating through the crowd. The voice had not grabbed his attention. "Uncle, Uncle!" The shout finally registered in his mind. Kumar! He dared not turn! He would blame the noise around for not having heard.

"Uncle, it's me Kumar!" Kumar shouted as he saw the old man squeeze hastily through the crowd. Not sure if he had been heard Kumar tried to catch up. But it was difficult to rush through a packed lane. Hawkers were positioned on both sides of the street. Shoppers flooded the remaining space. Just as Kumar saw a gap in the crowd to hasten the chase he saw his benefactor get into an auto.

"D. N. Road!" shouted the elder, breathlessly. He cursed Kumar. The auto ride was out of character and an additional expense. This act of cowardliness shook his confidence. He was proud of his direct nature. He never ran away from situations. He had barely resigned himself to the loss of money. Kumar's audacity to accost him again was unnerving. No more parting of his hard earned money to fund someone's questionable life! To err was human but to repeat it would be stupid.

He rushed into his house. He spluttered the incident to his wife expecting moral support. Instead, the reaction was a combination of 'I-told-you-so' and 'look-what-you-have-got-into'. Just then the doorbell rang. They both looked at each other. They somehow guessed who was at the door. "I am not at home!" said the very exasperated man running towards the bathroom. "Ok. I will deal with this," he heard his wife assure him.

He sat on an overturned bucket wondering how the situation had reached this tragi-comic state. He had been one of the few capable men entrusted by his company to handle occasional agitations by the labour workforce. His life had involved tense situations manfully handled. But here he was avoiding a broken young man in his own home! Was it guilt of having to say no or was it the shame of having been taken advantage of? Was it softness of heart brought by old age? He stared at nothing in particular as his ears strained to hear what was being said outside. He heard the front door slam shut and then a knock on the bathroom door.

"I hope this doesn't become a daily affair," he groaned. "Don't worry my gallant knight," his wife teased with affection. "I told him you were at a friend's place and would return late. I also told him that you've taken up a temporary assignment and would not be home during the day. So he should call before coming over. That'll give you a head start. I asked him whether he had any message but he preferred to talk to you." She couldn't resist a chuckle. It was rare to see him on his back foot. But underneath the tough talk was deep affection for her husband. She just had her own ways of expressing it.

In the following weeks Kumar tried to get in touch with the harried senior many times. But the phone in the house was rarely answered. If it was, his wife would be on the line with ready excuses - "Uncle is not at home" or "Uncle has just stepped out." Wanting some peace, the phone was kept off the hook for certain hours. Kumar was getting impatient. He had to meet Uncle desperately! At times he wondered if he was being avoided. But he didn't care. There had to be a way to contact the generous man. He decided to keep trying. That's the only thing he could do.

The calm benevolent man now spent most of the days worrying and in agitation. He stepped out of the house in dread and jumped every time the phone rang. He preached solving small problems before they became big. And here he was, unable to find a way out for himself. What should have been a few uncomfortable moments with Kumar had turned into a tangled mess stretching for days. The wise man knew that someday he would have to encounter Kumar. Adding to the awkwardness would be having to explain the evasions. Being a lousy liar, the old man knew that he would blurt out his true feelings and the distress caused to him.

Unable to handle the stress anymore the wary old man stopped going for his regular walks. As much as he could, he sent his wife to the market and endured her cribbing. He scanned the streets like a hunted man when he was forced to venture out. He became depressed and sulked often. "What a price we are paying for your good deed," his wife would mutter every time his mood darkened.

Finally one day, when he lost his temper at his wife for a trivial issue he realized that he had to break out of this before it cost them dearly. He decided to resume his walks and get back to his old self. Kumar be damned! What was he scared of? All this turmoil because of some guy with whom he had no relation, no obligation, no affiliation? For all he knew he might have already become history for Kumar.

That very evening the resolute old man went for a stroll. Friendly shopkeepers gave him polite nods. A few asked where he had been – they had missed seeing him in the evenings.

"Yes, I can understand what a long absence means for someone of my age," he joked. Along the way he had a hearty laugh with familiar faces. The affection accorded to him felt good. He was back to normal.

The Gulmohar trees welcomed him with their shade without fuss of his absence. He breathed in deeply - refreshed. He felt like a new man. Starve a man and a dish of raw vegetables becomes a feast.

He reached a ground where kids were enjoying this rare piece of free open space. People sat in groups.

Hovering around were hawkers selling balloons and roasted peanuts.

The senior citizen replayed the years spent in this area. There was a comforting gratitude in his heart. He closed his eyes and smiled to himself. These moments were what made life worth living.

"Uncle!" the unwelcome voice dragged him away from the blissful place. There was no escape this time. No way could he walk over the bushes, past the people, through the broken gates and out of earshot within seconds. He turned slowly towards the one who had destroyed his peace. His mind and body readied for the inevitable outburst. It was time to finish this story once and for all.

Kumar was standing before him, unchanged. He was a portrait of despair, depression and a lot of alcohol. "Uncle, I have found you at last!" He smiled triumphantly.

The good man's heart sank. He couldn't think of any important reason to rush off. Would he have to resort to rude rejection? "What is it, Kumar? I was just about to leave for home. There is some urgent work", he spoke tonelessly.

"Uncle I have been trying to meet you for so long."

"Yes, Yes, I was busy. What is it?"

"When I borrowed money from you that day, I was desperately in need of money. I know I promised to return it back in a few days. The thing is…." he hesitated. "I still need -"

"Listen Kumar," cut in the elderly man sternly. "That day, I gave you what I could. But please understand that I can't afford to help you financially. I live on my pension. I was caught off guard that day. But it's ok as a one-time thing. Your own friends don't want to lend you money. I was shocked to learn that they don't even want to associate with you anymore. Then what do you expect from me? Look at what you have done to yourself."

The response was a sad, tired smile. Kumar looked around the ground wondering how to take the conversation ahead.

"You are right in getting upset, Uncle," he said softly. "When someone is down in life, every negative aspect of his gets enhanced. Sadly, that's the only thing that people   notice. It is reassuring to see others worse than yourself, no? It overshadows your own troubles and faults. No one commented before when I drank regularly. Now, the only thing noticed is my appearance. And it's blamed on my drinking? Why don't they assume it could be due to stressful days and sleepless nights? Couldn't my shabby appearance be due to a distracted mind? My friends who judge me today were the first to desert me. Their lack of support added to my depression. I know what this sounds like. Like I am blaming everyone else for my troubles. But it's not so."

He gazed at a faraway point searching for the right words.

"You were the last resort after my own shunned me. I came to you with no expectations at all. It was just to complete the list of good people with whom I was comfortable. It was just a formality, Uncle. Hell, when your friends and family close the doors on you it is unrealistic to expect the kindness of others.

But I was surprised when you didn't hesitate to lend me money. Let me frankly admit. Not many would have done the same. Probably even I would not have. But what could I do when you handed me the money? Say no to the money that I had asked you for? I didn't know what to do at that time except take the money. I was deeply touched by this gesture of yours. No words can fully express the gratitude and respect that I have for you. You were the only one who showed some trust in me.

Uncle, I am still in a financial mess. I have heard the gossip about my situation – we all live in same locality after all. I don't need to justify myself to anyone. But let me assure you that my troubles are because of bad business decisions only. Not because of any vices. I don't deny that I made mistakes. The fault is all mine. So what? Had the gamble paid off my position would have been totally different. The Rs.2000 that you so kindly gave can't solve my crisis. But the confidence it instilled in me that day was priceless! I had to repay your faith in me by returning your money. No matter what! I am still in need of money. But your debt was more important than anything else. I owed it to my true self.

For the last few days I've been trying to contact you desperately. But you were unreachable. I didn't visit your house uninvited. Aunty told me to call before coming."

He put his hand in his pocket and brought out a wad of notes. He handed it to the elderly man. It was Rs.2000 in Rs.100 notes. Kumar then bowed slightly in respect.

"Uncle, I have returned the money as promised. I have cleared my dues. But I will always be indebted to you. Your trust in me will keep me motivated. Thanking you is not enough. I will wish you well forever."

With a tired smile that had a glow of its own Kumar walked away. The good hearted elderly gentleman was speechless for once. He put the money in his pocket. Money had never been given more importance than necessary. But the currency notes handed to him felt precious. He would never spend it.

The Classmate

In the early '90s I was studying at an engineering college in a small town. Like quite a few of such towns in India it had awakened to the business of education.Typically, the local bigwig politician acquired large acres of land and the approval to establish an educational institute. This would be under the umbrella of a charitable organization. Education as an industry would never run out of prospects in India where a college degree was not just a pathway to livelihood but also social acceptance. Demand exceeded supply in a country of a billion plus. No surprise then that my college too was sought after. A significant number of students were from outside the region.

When you are an outsider in a college dominated by local students you tend to associate mostly with similar outsiders. You spend time with your roommates. You hang out with friends in the canteen or on the streets. This is because you don't really belong there. You have no home to go to after college. There is an undercurrent of regional bias. So the city you came from determined whether the locals wanted to be friends with you or not.

There was nothing special about me. Nor did I excel at studies or extra-curricular activities. I was an average student living an ordinary life. My only USP was that I came from Mumbai - a fascination for the locals. Internet was yet to become a common utility. Mobile phones and malls were still to arrive. So it was generally believed that fast life existed only in the big cities. Guys from Mumbai would relate spicy stories of crime and Bollywood, apart from other stuff, which they claimed to be intimately aware of. I didn't do that sort of thing. This probably added to my image of being a genuinely cool guy. (A truly cool city guy would never need to give proof of it, would he?) And so fellow students sought my friendship and welcomed me in their circle. My good impression on them was purely unintentional.

However, there was one guy in my class who made quite an impression on me. He showcased a perspective of life I wouldn't have imagined existed, had I not met him.

He was fair, tall, medium built but leaning towards the heavier side and wore gold rimmed glasses. There was an air of aloofness about him which he never tried to do away with. Like an elephant who can't help but make its presence felt, he too stood out among us. But it was not due to his physical presence. He had an aura that was hard to miss.

There are the 'haves' and there are the 'have-nots'. Among the 'haves' if one studies closely, there are the well-off, the rich and the elite. The rich and the elite are well-off. All the elite are rich. But not all rich can be classified as elite in the real sense. The elite stand out with extra colors of heritage, background, sophistication born of upbringing and at times, a recognized family name. Add to all this is the tendency to not mingle much with the common class as much as they can help it. Sometimes it's by choice. Sometimes because, try as they might, they just don't gel well.

My elite classmate therefore could be forgiven for not really mixing with the crowd. That is if one assumed that he sought forgiveness. His audacity enhanced the reputation he had garnered at college. There was reluctant acceptance of what he was and what most other students could never be.

His attitude was of disdain. He didn't care a hoot for anyone. He had a weird habit of giving a short laugh in conversations, as if he found everything funny. It obviously got misinterpreted as his natural mocking nature. But he didn't do it out of spite or because he looked down on others. He was just being himself.

He commuted to college in his car or an expensive model of the Bullet bike. The envy of the audience was apparent though it was not his intention. A packet of Marlboro tucked in his shirt pocket would be visible to all. He didn't see anything wrong in it since most students smoked, though not openly. Students could afford only the local brands of cigarette, bought one at a time. He bought the full packet of the foreign brand because he could. He preferred having it at hand whenever he had the urge to light up. Sometimes he too would be found at the hotel frequented by students for their *'chai'* and a smoke. Looking for a seat, I would end up at the opposite side of his table which would invariably be empty. He would offer the

Marlboro to me. I would refuse. The brand was not in my league.

My early interactions with him were sparse but friendly. It would be one-liner conversations in English if we bumped into each other. His address to me mostly began with "Hey Bombaywalla!" Variations of this nickname was universal for students from this city though it had been renamed Mumbai not long ago. Maybe future students would get a different nickname. But for the current lot, the tag stuck.

Over the semesters we developed a casual friendship and the conversations lengthened. I got used to his mocking tone and the short laughs. Once I asked him about his plans after college. To my surprise he replied in his characteristic open nature that he would marry his girlfriend of many years. In the '90s, 'girlfriend', 'boyfriend' was still a hush-hush affair in India. So this was a pretty bold statement for someone living in a conservative region.

It was in our final year when he came up to me one day and said, "Hey Bombaywalla. What are you doing this Sunday?"

"I have a busy schedule doing nothing." My one- liner reply.

"Good," he said with a short laugh, "Come home for lunch."

Not prepared for this, I spluttered some excuse.

"Hey man, it's just lunch. Food. Made at home." He gave a knowing smile and raised his eyebrows up and down teasingly. Homemade food is a magnet for a hostel student. There was no use fighting the temptation.

That Sunday I set out for his home with mixed feelings. I tried to guess the reason for this sudden invitation. I was embarrassed about being the only one invited. I was the chosen one. Having heard so much about him and his background I wasn't sure of what was expected of me. I wore what I considered the best set of clothes a student living out of a suitcase might have. I thought of topics to talk with his parents and other family members. I could tell them juicy stuff about Mumbai. I felt the need to live up to the standards that they had. Thankfully my English was at par with the best. I could chatter away in polished English. Better still, I would shut up and talk as little as possible.

The rendezvous was a bus stop at the outskirts of a major town. It was an hour's ride from our college. A man waiting with a bike asked me whether I was the intended guest. I nodded. There couldn't have been two college students arriving at that junction from a rickety bus on a Sunday. I didn't tell him that though.

He gestured towards the bike. He would be taking me to the house. The journey took 15 minutes, passing fields and small houses. A sharp right into a path cut through rows of trees. I'm not much of nature watcher, so couldn't recognize the trees. Just that they were tall and thin. It was like riding through a forest. Soon there appeared a clearing. What lay ahead was impressive.

The three storied house was an old fashioned mansion. It was aged and aristocratic. The interior of the house began as a longish verandah with wooden benches on its sides. It seemed like a receiving area for general public. This led to another room whose purpose was unclear. Beyond that was the living room. It was as if the middle room was a buffer between the public and private zone of the house. The living room was huge and richly decorated. Large windows served as scenic background for rich furnishings. Artefacts were placed aesthetically around. Feeling self- conscious I maintained a cool demeanor to hide my awe of the surroundings.

My classmate was waiting. He greeted me with a big smile and a loud chuckle "So, you came at last. I thought you wouldn't find the way to my humble home."

The sarcasm was friendly and I smiled back. The preliminary small talk done with, he asked me to follow him. We climbed the stairs to the second floor. At the end of a long corridor was his bedroom. It was as large as a small flat in my city. We sat on cushioned chairs near the bedroom windows. The bedroom had a spacious balcony. From where I sat all I could see were trees.

"What's special today?" I asked.

"Nothing much," he smirked. "It's my Birthday."

"What are you saying man!" I reacted sharply. "You could have at least told me before, *yaar*. I would have got something. At least a card. This is so embarrassing. Anyways …..Happy Birthday. My best wishes for a great life ahead. I mean it."

"Hey relax Bombaywalla!" he used the nickname to tease me. He gave a short laugh. "I'm not into birthday cards, gifts. All that stuff. I meant to invite you one of these days anyways. You never know if we will meet after this semester. The birthday was just a coincidence. And I'm sure the gifts I want are a little beyond your monthly budget." He laughed heartily at his own joke. I didn't retort with the clichéd "it-is-the-thought-that-counts". It would have sounded pathetic.

We were engrossed chatting about the college days gone by when there was a polite knock on the open door of the bedroom. A fair petite lady with a pleasant smile stood outside. She must have been in her twenties. When he acknowledged her, she came over. With a pleasant formality she handed him a birthday card. He accepted it with thanks. He didn't introduce her and I didn't ask. You never knew how touchy one was about the ladies of the family.

We returned to the living room to be introduced to his elegant father who fit the profile of the sophisticated squire. He had an air of aristocratic regency. He indulged me with the right amount of small talk required of courtesy and took his leave. After a quick tea we went to the third floor which had a few rooms and a large rooftop terrace. There was a mini – refrigerator (never seen one in a house before) probably containing soft drinks. At the centre of the terrace was a set of expensively cushioned cane furniture.

Soon his friends arrived – three girls and two guys. Two of the three girls were fair and beautiful. They had an air of silent arrogance. It reeked of snobbish high class upbringing. They gave me enough attention not to appear aloof but not enough to be friendly. Their demeanor gave the message that they were being polite just because I was amidst them. There were subtle signals that they had no interest in me, neither as a friend nor as an acquaintance for the future. Since one of these two had to be his girlfriend, I saw it prudent to keep my distance too. The guys also had the similar attitude. Birds of a feather did flock together. As time passed I mentally switched off to them.

Strangely, the third girl didn't fit in this group. She had dark skin, was average looking and wore ordinary glasses with her simple dress. Had she not been with them it would have been hard to believe that she was a part of the snob group. But what she lacked in looks was overcompensated by her personality. She was pleasant and had a sense of humour. She took efforts to make me feel comfortable. She took initiative during the get-together. She was the one ensuring that everyone participated in the conversations.

But I knew my place and maintained a polite presence. My only incentive had been the home cooked food. The delicious varieties took my undivided attention. It was worth every moment of alienation that I was feeling. My mind wandered as an escape from this group. I marveled at the vastness of the house. It must have been built for a large joint family. But now it seemed to be inhabited by hardly anyone. Apart from this lot, I had only seen a young woman and his father. Where was his mother? Would she be as graciously formal as his father had been? Was his mother one of those socialites who had no time for family or motherhood? Was he pampered because he was the only son? Was he a loner because he had probably lost his mother as a child? Any of these reasons could explain his personality he was famous for at college.

By late afternoon the friends took leave, addressing me with their insincere smiles and superficial farewells. Only the simple looking girl had a genuine smile because it reached her eyes. She hoped that we would meet again though we both knew it would not be so.

There was still time for me to catch the town bus. So my classmate asked me to hang around with him instead of waiting at the bus stop. We sat by an artificial pond in a garden, a few minutes' walk behind the house. There was a statue of a mermaid in the middle of the pond. The water shimmered in the breeze.

"So how did you like my little world? Did you have a good time?" he asked, taking out a cigarette. "Interesting. Very fulfilling. The food was awesome," I replied sincerely.

"Yes. Maybe home food feels that way if you don't get it daily," he said with a twinkle in his eyes. "So what did you think of my girlfriend? Remember I told you once about my plans after college? My very soon 'to-be wife'"?

I remained silent, not wanting to reply without a thought. I wasn't sure which of the two pretty girls he was talking about. They both fit his type. And no way would I tell him my true opinion of them. But he was looking at me intently for an answer.

"Good choice," I muttered in an even tone. "Pretty to look at and interesting to talk to." The 'pretty' was true. The 'interesting-to-talk-to' was just to make him feel good. The girls had not graced me with their beauty or their brains.

Hearing this he began to laugh. Much to my surprise it was not his customary short laugh. In fact, he laughed so hard for a while that he had to remove his glasses to wipe his tears.

Wiping the glasses he smirked, "You're like the rest of the world after all. Not that I blame you."

"I don't understand. Did I say something to offend you? I didn't mean to, man. I'm sorry if I said something wrong."

"No *yaar*! Don't be silly," he reassured me with a friendly pat on the shoulder. "But tell me, just out of curiosity, why did you pick those two? Why did you leave out the other one? You know ....Thin, dark, ordinary, with glasses, with a non-Brahmin surname. The one not from a rich family." His words were laced with bitter sarcasm.

So this was what they called a rhetorical question. He had already listed the answers in his question. They were the universally accepted parameters for judging a person's worth.

Inwardly embarrassed, I didn't say a word. For all my cosmopolitan upbringing, I had followed the same bullshit reasoning as anyone else. The thought of looking beyond the obvious had not even crossed my mind. It was not so much about guessing the right one among the three. How many would have considered the ordinary girl as an option?

Seeing my awkwardness he spoke to fill in the silence. "It's ok. Don't feel so bad. I would have been bloody surprised if you had picked the right one!"

His familiar chuckle told me it was alright.

"We are childhood friends. We were in the same school, same tuition classes. She would have been in our college if it had a computer engineering department. You know, we became friends without any effort. We became close without any intention. Isn't that the real deal? For a fish, the water should seem a natural part of its existence. The day it sees itself separate from the water is the day it is out of the water. And that's the end." He paused. "That was so filmy. Like you, Bombaywalla," he chuckled. "We plan to marry within a year. College degree and marriage degree in one year itself! *Phataphat!*"

"Your parents ok with it?"

"Yes they are. It's not as if they can do anything about it. You met them today, see."

"I met your father," I said. "Umm…. your mother….. I didn't see her," I added cautiously.

He looked at me and simply said, "Yes you have. She was the lady you met first."

I was speechless! That young, petite, twenty-something woman was his mother? What strange people. My confusion was quite visible. I must have gone red in embarrassment because he smiled and said, "Relax. She is my step- mother. My father's second wife."

I knew I had to say something. My inability to respond enhanced the awkwardness. "I am sorry," I blurted.

"For what?"

To have a step-mother meant only two things. His mother must have passed away or his parents were divorced. I chose a safe statement applicable to both the scenarios. "For your loss." My confused emotions tried to sound genuinely sympathetic.

"Ah! It's not that tragic," he dismissed with a wave. "My parents are divorced, that's all. My mother lives in a city few hours from here."

"But it must be tough for you," I countered, irritated at his casualness. Did his sense of superiority refuse courteous comfort from anyone?

"Why does the world insist on creating slots? Why are lives sorted into categories?" he asked no one in particular.

Pointing beyond the pond he asked, "Can you see those plants out there? And that tree?"

I looked searchingly in the direction.

"Yes….. That tree. It's a mango tree," he informed helpfully.

I nodded finally.

"We have a gardener who tends to them. What do you think is the real role of a gardener?"

I waited for him to continue. I had got the hang of rhetoric questions.

His smile this time was pleasant, as if coming from the heart. Not out of habit but because he wanted to. This was a rare moment. He was revealing his inner self to someone not of his inner world. Had he sensed a kinship with me all these years? Did he have a depth of maturity that he had not been given credit for?

"We want our plants and trees to be healthy and so we nurture them. In return, we expect them to give us what we want," he continued. "Flowering plants should have lovely flowers. The mango tree should give us mangoes every year. Plants and trees should add beauty to the place. A gardener will be appreciated if it happens. But if this does not happen, we are disappointed. The gardener might be even blamed for not taking good care. But is he really responsible for the flowering and the bearing of fruits?" He paused. "You think I am going tangent?"

"A little," I admitted.

He gave a short laugh.

"I know you don't know what the hell I am talking about. For a guy like you nature talk must be boring. But I'm trying to give you a broader perspective of my situation. It will be clear soon. And of course you get the benefit of my deep wisdom." There was humour in his voice. I gave a mock bow of respect. He laughed and continued.

"See, the true role of a gardener is to nurture. His job is to take care of the plants. Do whatever it takes for their well-being. Water them, add soil and manure. Stuff like that. At times even cut a branch or a stem. As long as they are healthy it should not matter if there are fruits or flowers. Only those who really love nature will understand this. Most people pass judgements on the basis of fruits and flowers. The *external* signs, the tangible rewards. My family has learnt to think like the gardener. Do you see where I'm going?"

He paused, giving me time to take it all in.

"Ok. Let me tell you what I really mean," he said. "Do you see all the land around us?

"I couldn't miss it even if I tried," I muttered.

"Ha! Ha! Yes," he laughed. "My forefathers were typical feudalistic landlords. Along with the land, the harvests, and the livestock, you could say that they unofficially owned the people as well. Obviously, that kind of control doesn't exactly exist anymore. But the mindset is still there in some form or other. Like mingling only with similar families, control over lands and businesses, connections with the powerful. You know, that sort. Quite a lot of people here still work in companies and lands owned by a few such families.

And there are the pleasures. Women, gambling, hunting, to name a few obvious ones. The few who don't indulge are tolerant of those who do. Some facilitate it for their vested interests. No one is above it. I'm sure you've heard of men who don't drink but have a well-stocked bar. So there are no judgments in our circle. They are in it in some way or the other. Outside our world it does not matter. We never hear about it upfront anyways."

He paused to light himself another smoke. There was relief in his expression.

"My father is a perfect fit. He has always lived an aristocratic lifestyle. It is natural to him. He is close to his family, but in a form that allows no emotional bonding. Like the men of his kind, his other interests are discreet but not a secret. So what surprised us was his need to make it legal and public. This decision of his a few years back, has changed our lives.

My mother is from a rich family herself. She was raised in a cosmopolitan atmosphere of a city. But she was married off at a young age to this family here. You can imagine her situation. Her heart was never here. She would go to her hometown at every opportunity. It's not too far. Only about four hours by car. All her close friends live there. Over the years, I could sense the distance between my parents. It had become a marriage of duty. She became numb as a person. Her confident outward personality was just a mask for the world. And there were no serious issues to justify a divorce.

That was until my father's decision to go separate ways. My mother didn't hesitate to grab the chance of a lifetime. She is now happily divorced, living life on her terms. She got her freedom and her share of the assets. She also gets to play the wronged woman - the victim. She has lots of support. Now she is one of the trustees of a high profile women's association. It's given her a purpose in life.

It was a win-win situation. Funnily, they are now closer as friends - two people with affection but no obligations. Whenever asked she is there to guide my step – mother in the matters of the house."

He stopped for any comments from me. I didn't say anything. He appreciated the gesture and continued.

"I have an elder brother. He was the unquestioned heir to the family. He is intelligent, dynamic. Some say the image of my grandfather himself. So you can imagine the importance he commanded. But he was totally disinterested in staying here. He studied in one of the best boarding schools in the country. Most of his childhood was spent away from us. You can see why he had no real bond with anyone here. Not with family or friends. He couldn't relate to this place or the people. His dream was to settle down in the US. Growing up he spent his vacations travelling the world. It was as if he wanted to stay away as much as possible till he had no choice but to take over from father. He was allowed all his excesses except that of settling away from home. After all, he had been groomed to be the next in line. In return for acquiescing to father's decision to remarry he was allowed his demands. He went to the US to study further and is comfortably placed there. He has got his share of the family wealth. To ensure his permanency he has married an American. Knowing him, he must have married the first woman to agree to his proposal."

Taking a pebble from the ground he casually flung it in the pond.

"That leaves me," he said with a long breathe. "I'm the average one in the family. When you've a brother like mine you get overshadowed without really being meant to. I am, what you can say, a truly local lad. I love this place and will never leave my town. My whole life has been spent here. I plan to spend the rest of my life here too. I was to be a second to my brother in running our businesses. Nothing much was expected of me and I was left alone. I would have been married to someone of our status just as it would have been for my brother. Marriage is a great excuse to foster business and lineage alliances. There was no compromise on that. There is an unspoken acceptance of getting what you want through other means. Then why waste a strategic option like marriage?

You see where this is going, don't you? Father had no choice but to make me the heir. I've control over most of the family business. Two of our companies are in my name now. The rest will be mine after my father. And a man who has a wife near about his son's age has no say in his son's choice of a wife. Whatever her background and looks. So there is green signal for my marriage as well. With the one you forgot to add in your list. My first gift to her after marriage is gold rimmed glasses. Then we will be a perfect match!"

With that he gave a hearty laugh. It was of relief and happiness in sharing his story. He gave me a friendly pat. I know the gesture meant good wishes for me which he wouldn't say aloud. It was also probably thanks for an unexpected chance to speak from the heart. Something I assume, he had not done before. We both looked at the pond ahead in silence. When he spoke again there was a pleasant ring to it which I doubt I had heard before.

"We've all made our peace with the situation. We are definitely not close to my father's wife. But we don't hate her nor grudge her anything. She is an integral presence in our lives. We have given her the respect accordingly.

From society's point of view, we have gone through a big crisis. In a town like ours, this is definitely a big scandal. It will be yet another story about our family. And there will be *masala* added. But only we know that the new member of our family has been a positive omen. Her entry has untangled the hopeless issues and set us all free.

Society might see a tree with no fruits, a plant with no flowers. But we know that our family tree has been nurtured and that it will grow."

The Woman and the Little Girl

My first job was in the marketing department of an MNC in India. As a fresher the initial months had to be spent in a rural region. Experienced managers didn't want a rural transfer, least of all in the interiors of the country. New recruits had to accept these unpopular postings. This was packaged as a good learning experience for the newbies.

Thus barely out of college, my career began in a small village whose local language I could speak. Villages were allotted as per knowledge of the local language. This was to ensure smooth communication with the locals. Language barrier could not be an excuse for poor performance.

The company provided for the stay, travel and food expenses. It was a fixed amount irrespective of the actual expenditure. If smartly budgeted, the money could be utilized effectively.

For travelling professionals on a company payroll, these reimbursements are very important. It gives them the confidence to go the extra mile and concentrate on work without worrying about their pockets. It serves as a sort of a perk. Many use this to earn an extra buck through smart management. A simple example is when money provided for a cab is used for public transport and the difference is pocketed. Of course, not everyone does it. Some believe in squeezing out all the comforts accorded by their company – not readily affordable on their own. To each his own.

As a young man starting out in life, comfort was not as important as a little extra money, however small the amount. I calculated the money that could be saved from the expense account. The major expense turned out to be accommodation. So I decided to look for a place which served my three B's- Bag-Bath-Bed. A room for my belongings, for freshening up and for shelter. That was all the comfort I needed.

Being young makes you adventurous. I wanted to experience simplistic living. It would be something to solemnly brag about to my friends in the city. And who knows? If I ever moved up the corporate world, this would be an experience to 'humbly' relate. The leader who began his illustrious career from grassroots level. From this perspective living a villager's life seemed appealing.

Eventually I found such a place in the village. In a local's house, a room was up for rent. The lodge in the village would have been ideal. But staying with this family would save considerable amount of money. The room catered to one or two day stays and was priced accordingly. The cost difference between the simple room and the lodge was substantial. It took a lot of convincing for the villager to agree. He was not sure whether his family and his house matched up to my profile. But I had made up my mind to stay there. The elderly villager reluctantly agreed. If this city lad wanted the rustic life, who was he to refuse?

The house though, was not the quintessential village dwelling. It looked as if it had been built in stages, depending on the availability of money or material. Every possible buildable area was used so far and provisions were made for future construction. There were concrete pillars jutting out at the top. More importance had been given to utility than aesthetics. The entrance was a large, thick wooden door which opened into a short dark passage. This led to a small courtyard, open to the sky. Surrounding it were rooms on three sides. At the fourth side was a wooden staircase of broken uneven steps. This led to an upper floor consisting of a room and an external bathroom.

The room was small, just enough to squeeze in a bed and a table. Presumably, the space under the bed was the storage area for bags. The room was not meant for comfort, but convenience for a short stay. A small window high on the wall provided ventilation but not ample daylight. A door at the other end of the room opened to a surprisingly wide balcony, overlooking a terrace. The terrace was accessible only from the house below. There was hardly any gap between the balcony and the terrace. The balcony had a chair. This was where you sat for light and fresh air.

I was not discomforted by this setting, finally understanding the reluctance of the owner. Under different circumstances, I would have never stayed here. For the present though, I had reasons to convince myself of its advantages.

Slowly but steadily, I settled down to a routine. I left the house at around 10 am keeping in mind the slow pace of the place. I returned by 5 pm even though work got over earlier. There was nothing to do in my room to pass the time. Internet, smart phones and such were yet to drastically alter the existing social life. Within a week, my curiosity about village life was satiated. There were no places to aimlessly linger around. I found ways to somehow spend time till 5 pm. That became my deadline. On weekends, I travelled to a town half an hour away for a movie and food at a relatively better hotel. There I could safely have a drink instead of the village shack. Every fortnight required me to visit the regional office two hours away by road. I kept count of the days for my return to the city to begin my career in earnest.

Whenever possible I chose the comfort of the airy balcony over the room. There was nothing to see except the bare terrace of the house. Sitting outside, I made 'to do' lists in the morning, read a book on a holiday afternoon and enjoyed the evening and night breeze. The only book I had was "A Concise History of The Modern World" By W. Woodruff. I loved reading world history and had space for only one book to take me through my tenure. This thick book satisfied all parameters.

The household consisted of the villager, his wife, their son and his wife and a little girl. The elderly couple, in their late sixties, had a kind and pleasant demeanor. After the initial awkwardness, the old villager was eager to be a good landlord and took efforts to make me comfortable. The son, in his late thirties, had the rugged look of a rough rural life. He was bulky and kept a shabby beard. He was polite when he spoke, which was rarely. It was not out of rudeness though. He was conscious in my presence and there wasn't much to talk anyways. We belonged to different worlds. The family owned a small patch of farm. The son also ran a grocery shop in the village.

I saw the wife a few days after my arrival. I was surprised to find her so young. I had assumed her to be around the same age as her husband. But she was in her early twenties, no doubt married off very early. She was fairly good looking. She had a slender petite body with light brown skin and silky hair. Strands of hair would fall at the side of her face, which she would gracefully tuck behind her ear.

Her attractiveness, I realised, was because of her allure and not physical beauty. It was heightened by the way she carried herself and the way she dressed. Her *sari* though worn traditionally had a "blink-of-second" sexiness. Women instinctively pulled the *pallu* of the *sari* across their chest and midriff if they felt exposed. But the young wife never did so when I happened to be around. Was the lack of reflex action because she was used to having only her family in the house? Was it ignorance of a village girl unaware of the ways of the world? Or was it something else?

So I often got a glimpse of her midriff. She had the best hips I had seen in a long time. Her slight paunch deepened her navel, which drew my attention to it like iron to a magnet. What chance did a young guy have against such distractions? Once in a while, when she sat on the floor of the courtyard, her perky breasts would seek my attention. She had that 'carefully-careless' way about her that was very seductive. Careful enough not to cross any limits. Careless enough to be bold in a seemingly unintentional way.

Not that we encountered each other much. It was hardly for a few minutes and that too not every day.

We came across each other only in the courtyard, either on my way up to my room or my way down. She would greet me with a demure smile of a good host. Her gaze indicated a personality which lay suppressed. We never spoke. Knowing my place in the house and the prevalent social environment, I never sought to make conversation nor linger anywhere near her.

With her little daughter it was different though. She was around 4 years old and cute, like all kids of that age. (Even her coarse father must have looked cute as a 3 year old.) Little kids are either shy or very friendly around strangers. They have not yet formed inhibitions or preconceived judgements. The girl was refreshingly friendly. She brought charm and liveliness to the drab interiors of the house. She was as if an external personification of her mother's true nature. She would either be playing by herself or be in the arms of her mother or the grandparents. Every morning as I left for work I found the little girl in the courtyard. It was probably the only safe open space for the kid to play. On seeing me she would run to me expecting a friendly response. Initially I only smiled back, conscious about interacting with the family too much. It was a conservative village after all. Better to be safe than sorry.

However her innocence won me over in a week. One morning, as I looked at the cute face, I spoke without realizing. "Good morning," I said automatically in English. It was the language I was most comfortable in.

The little girl's eyes widened with surprise. She gave an excited giggle. Obviously she had not understood what I had said. The look on her face was priceless. It brightened my day just thinking of it.

When I returned in the evening she came over and I said, "Good evening." The foreign sounds amused her again. And returning from dinner, the ever present girl was greeted with a 'Good night.' The response was the same - glee and wonderment. No hesitation in expressing herself and no superficiality. Her reactions lifted my mood and made me happy.

This was the bright spark in a dull environment. A flicker of a candle did brighten a dark cave. The earlier resolve was modified in her case. I decided to carry on this little conversation with the little girl.

There wasn't anything wrong in it. This didn't count as being too friendly. And it was always in the open courtyard where her family kept a watchful eye.

So began greetings from my end and wide eyed responses from her end. 'Good morning' to begin the day and 'Good night' to end the day. There was an occasional 'Good evening' and 'Good afternoon'. The little girl was thrilled with this new play. At times she ran back to whoever was present and talked animatedly in her mother tongue. I didn't converse in her language because a part of me was still cautious about stepping too far. So our connect was restricted to those few sentences in English for a few minutes of the day.

While a distant bond was forming with the little girl over time, I started noticing curious behavior on her mother's part.

The young woman's mannerisms and dress sense would have caught any man's fancy. When she revealed herself in small ways it added to her seductiveness. Her midriff with the enticing navel, the almost bare back above the curvy hips and the perky breasts were always at the back of my mind. Once you have seen something it cannot be unseen. And memories make it as fresh as the actual moment.

This further frustrated the lonely me. I spent the days with rustic men of the villages and the evenings with my own miserable self. An occasional glimpse of the petite woman naturally brought out unavoidable emotions. A tree in a forest is just a part of the scenery. But a single blade of grass in the desert stands out. The effect is heightened by its presence and by what it represents. She was that grass. But she was also a mirage − pleasant upfront but an unpleasant afterthought.

So it was with mixed feelings that I started noticing the subtle signals.

In the initial days she would smile politely, a basic civility conferred on anyone familiar. Over time however, the smile and the gaze lingered for seconds longer than I had come to expect. Nothing odd about it on its own. But in perspective it stood out for further comprehension.

The social environment in the village was pretty conservative. In brutal honesty, it could be called regressive. One rarely saw guys and girls together in public. If they were together, they were related. In fact, I hardly saw young women alone in public, even at the markets. Women were either with family or in the company of other women. The young wife's smile in some other place could be called friendly and not given much thought. But considering the existent social backdrop, "friendly" was bold and brash for a woman.

After a few such encounters I got disconcerted every time we came across each other. Though I would smile back politely I was very uncomfortable. I wanted no problems because of this woman's sudden need to be social. A successful career in the company was more important. I warned myself repeatedly not to get carried away. The need for a female companion in my loneliness was probably making me read too much into it.

One day as I sat in the balcony, a sight further raised my suspicions. On the previously bare terrace, there was now a clothesline. On it hung a young woman's clothing. And worse, among them were two sets of a woman's underwear. You didn't have to be an expert in female garments to know that it was neither a little girl's nor of an old woman. Embarrassed, I quickly stepped into my room and closed the door. If I sat there I would be staring straight in that direction. There was nowhere else to look.

I was fuming with racy thoughts. I tried to make sense of it. The petite underwear had aroused me for sure. There are no constraints to a man's visualization of a woman. And when there are visual aids, imagine the torrent of images! Did the pretty designs reflect personal taste? Or was it an involuntary selection based on availability and cost?

Was the damsel sending me stronger hints? Had she assumed I had missed the subtle ones and was being forceful? When the excitement in my heart and pants normalized I began to analyze it differently. This could be a one-off incident. There might not have been space where she normally dried her clothes. Or maybe she had got used to my presence after all these months. Familiarity had made her comfortable enough to resume drying clothes where she used to. Since it was a usual practice to dry clothes on the terrace, she didn't expect anyone to give it attention.

These reasons sounded plausible if taken individually. But as a sequence of events, other possibilities could not be discounted.

Unfortunately, it was not a one-off thing. She continued drying her clothes occasionally on the terrace. Her underwear was a consistent item irrespective of other clothes. Reluctantly, I decided not to sit in the balcony if her clothes were on the clothesline. But unable to resist, I would take a long look at them before quickly closing the door.

While that was happening in the background, the days thankfully retained its happy routine. The little girl would be greeted in English without fail.

"Good morning," I smiled to her as I set off to work one morning.

"Gud mani," she replied beaming with pride.

Had she just spoken back? I had turned to walk on but her reply halted me. Turning back to her I repeated, "Good morning."

"Gud mani," She repeated.

I could have hugged her in joy! She had picked up her first words in English! And that too from me!

I was elated the whole day, thinking only of the morning's episode. That evening I bought her a chocolate after taking permission from her father. He agreed with a plain smile. I didn't want to make it a habit of buying her chocolates but she deserved the reward.

My sense of achievement soared when in the next few weeks her vocabulary included "Gud mani" "Gud noo" "Gud evnee" and "Gud nai."

I was proud of myself. This was becoming the highlight of the trip. My work was being appreciated at the head office. Was that not the goal? But somehow it didn't match the glow I felt about the little girl's progress. When it would be time to learn English, she would be way ahead of the class. Obviously she would not remember me when she grew older. But I would know my contribution and that's what really mattered. I planned to buy some books of basic English. But I would hand it over only on the day I was leaving. I didn't want the family to feel obliged during my stay. They showed quite a lot of deference anyways.

The elderly couple frequently enquired about my comforts while their son was friendly within his capabilities. The wife was making me feel special in her own way. But nothing could beat the joy the little girl brought.

Eventually I added more lines to the kiddy conversation. After her response to the greetings of the day, I would say, "How are you? Fine?" She listened attentively knowing it was something new to grasp. I waited eagerly for the day when she would repeat the lines in kid version. Motivated by her interest, the English conversations had moved up a notch. I was excited at her progress. However she was blissfully unaware of the positive effect on me. For the little one it was just play.

I was sitting in the balcony one day after making sure that there were no clothes hanging outside. Suddenly, I saw the young woman walk onto the terrace with a bucket. She smiled at me with the gaze I was now very familiar with. I didn't know what to do? Leaving abruptly would be rude and my not-so-innocent thoughts might become obvious. *Where was that damn book*! It was on the table in the room. It would have served as an excuse to look down and been an effective distraction too. I promised to bang my head against it later - a deserving punishment for being taken off guard.

The clotheslines covered the length of the terrace. Turning my head away was useless. And for how long can you stare at the sky arcing your neck? Reluctantly I looked ahead. She picked up one item at a time from the bucket on the floor. She would squeeze out the water, open the clothing, shake it in the air and place it on the rope.

I tried hard not to pay attention, but failed miserably. She was in her full glory. Bathed in sunlight, every part of her body shone crystal clear. The private wear of a woman, getting a thorough treatment would undoubtedly draw attention, wouldn't it? If that was not enough, the lady herself was titillating in her gestures. At times she faced me while hanging the clothes. The navel of her soft bare stomach invited me mockingly. Her breasts played hide and seek with the *pallu* - more 'seek' than 'hide', from my point of view. And when she turned her back towards me all I noticed was that it led to a firm behind. The spicing on the cake (it couldn't have been icing – it was hot!) were her movements during the whole time. The bending to pick up the clothes, the arcing of arms to place the clothes, the jumping of breasts when she roughly flicked the clothes in the air.

Arousal at such close quarters was frustrating. It was cruel and unfair! I tried to hopelessly suppress the uncontrollable passion within me. When my mind flashed her naked body in a frenzy of animalistic lust, I thought of boring stuff like Maths to 'de-lustify' myself. When my mind enviously cursed her lucky husband, to distract it, I recollected events in that bloody book which had deserted me. Every ecstasy filled image of hers was forcefully replaced by ugly or dull stuff to neutralize the effect.

One of the bras slipped out of her wet hands. She turned to see if I had noticed her carelessness and giggled self-consciously. At that moment yet another version of her was apparent - a damsel still on her path to womanhood.

At what age had she been married off? At what age had she become a mother? How motherly was that mother who was in need of mothering herself? How many unfulfilled desires did she have? Was my presence triggering a wish of fulfilling some of them?

I couldn't sleep that night and tossed around restlessly. *Why was she behaving like this? Where was this leading?* Ordinary people have had flings with celebrities (even the two-bit famous ones), no matter age or looks. They did so because they ended up getting an opportunity to sleep with a 'personality' not accessible to just about anyone. The bragging rights were priceless. *Were her seductions, a village woman's desire for something inaccessible, like a city guy?* City folks didn't land up in this nowhere of a village, did they? I had been offered to her literally at her doorstep. This was her 'once-in-her-lifetime' chance for a private unique experience.

I had mentally prepared myself to a mundane life in a sleepy village. It was unbelievable that in a single house I had found two females affecting me profoundly! I couldn't wait for my tenure to end. After

214

pondering over it deeply, I resolved to tackle the issues in a proactive and practical manner.

With regards to the little girl there was no doubt. I would continue the English lessons. Maybe increase the words to hasten her grasp and maximize our short interactions. As planned I would give her books on the last day. If possible I would sponsor English tuitions after I left. Her current nursery school didn't teach English.

As for the young woman, the matter had to be handled delicately. It was sensible to avoid her totally. Out of sight and out of mind. I could pretend to be in a serious mood or deep in thought whenever we encountered each other. I would not meet her gaze. This would eliminate the need to smile. I decided not to look at her, especially the enticing parts. This would keep my emotions in check.

Another idea was desirable but idiotic. I could tell her in private, her effect on me. I would clarify that there was no ulterior motive in letting her know about it. Then wait for her response. Embarrassed by her unintentional influence she would apologize, and it would stop. Or, she would confess that it was intentional. We would then get into bed whenever we got the chance. Whatever the response, she was not stupid to relate our conversation to anyone – especially her husband. I knew enough of the family and the village to be sure of that. But just to be on the safe side, I decided to find an alternate place to stay before taking any action.

I obviously opted for the safer option - that of avoidance. I resolved not to get too excited about her. Discretion was the better part of valour – of which I had little. But it was easier said than done. After experiencing a deeper level of intimacy it was difficult to backtrack to surface level civility. Every time we met in the courtyard, my mind flashed back to the terrace seduction. But the wish to teach the little girl was stronger than the need to avoid the woman. Quite often talking with the girl meant being in the presence of her mother. And my resolve would drown in a whirlpool of fantasy.

A few weeks later during a casual chat, the old landlord mentioned that his son was going out of town for a few days. Suddenly I was keen on the second option - that of talking to the woman. So far I had never spoken a word to her. Now, I contemplated initiating it. But doubts on whether it was a smart move refused to go away.

The dilemma was resolved the day before the son was to leave. The relief though was replaced by shock. I was lazing in the balcony late in the evening when I saw the woman run up the terrace with a bucket. It was an odd time to dry clothes. To my utter surprise she dashed to the edge of the terrace which almost touched the balcony.

She spoke hurriedly in a hushed voice, "My husband is going out of town. I will meet you tomorrow in your room at 5 pm. Please be there!" She then raced to the clothesline, quickly placed two clothes on it and ran down.

I didn't get time to reply. But it wasn't a question, was it? She hadn't asked whether we could meet but simply stated that we were to meet. The decision that I had been deliberating for so long had been taken by her. There was no doubt now that her desire if not greater, was equal to mine.

I paced up and down in excitement in that closet of a room. So it was finally happening! Like in movies and erotic stories - the village nymphet seducing the man from the city. Apparently, flings with local women did happen on out of town trips, if one believed the tales told. But was it so easy and could it happen to anyone? To be honest, it was only by sheer luck and nothing else that I was to be a part of that small percentage that did have such experiences. This was one extra feather in my tales for the years ahead.

Pacing back and forth I decided to view this development dispassionately. I didn't want to make a fool of myself on that day. She had shown cleverness. Those intelligent looks did have a mind to match. She had waited patiently all these days for an ideal opportunity to make our liaison.

Every evening, the old couple followed a routine. They visited the community center to meet friends. They usually left after tea at around 4:30 pm and returned not later than 6:30 pm. They frequently took the little girl along. The young woman would be left alone in the house for two hours at the most. Occasionally, the husband would pop in for tea before leaving for his shop again. Tomorrow, with the husband gone, she would be alone for sure. In all my days there she had never stepped on the staircase leading to my room. What was the need? Forget being in the room or on my floor. Even seen on the staircase would have been enough to raise all sorts of questions. Tomorrow she could do as she pleased in that one hour that had been gifted to her. 5 pm was perfect.

I planned to do as much as possible in her company. I fantasised moves that would give greater pleasure in the short time we had. Spend more time in foreplay and then finish it off quickly? Have quick sex first before fate had second thoughts? A slogan came to mind - 'Eat dessert first, life is too short'. Whatever the choices, one thing was for sure. Whether we had sex or not, I would definitely want to see her in the nude. It was my minimum benchmark for a time well spent. The memory of her naked body would stay with me forever. To be enjoyed whenever the desire arose.

My pragmatic mind considered the situation from other angles as well. I would be on my guard for any hidden motives behind this meeting. I wanted a good time with no strings attached. Literally and metaphorically! There were other reasons for seduction other than 'magnetic attraction'. So there could be no demands for money, love, wanting to run away to the city or such things.

To be on the safe side, I willed myself not to make the first move. Neither in words nor in action. She would have to make the first move. She would have to tell me what she wanted us to do. She would have to strip herself. At least start the undressing and I would definitely hasten it. It had to be a memorable experience for both of us. Pleased with my strategy I slept in anticipation of the next day.

The day arrived and I was ready for it even before the sun was. The husband had an early morning bus to catch. I sat in the balcony in the cold dawn. Faint sounds of the household readying for his trip could be heard.

Later the little girl met me in the courtyard. Her mother was not around. Probably just as conscious as me. Or was it guilt?

"Good morning."

"Good moni," a big cheerful smile spoke. She could now utter 'good' correctly.

"How are you? Fine?" I continued, not paying the usual attention. My mind was auto set on the evening ahead.

"Yooo Faeee" she replied earnestly.

The hours passed in a daze. It felt like the days when the exam results were due. There was nothing you could do about it at present yet all your being had moved to that point in future. Your mind already lived the moment a thousand times in anxiety and anticipation.

I postponed a meeting scheduled for early afternoon to the next day. I didn't want to be late even though there would have been ample time. I rushed to my room early, at around 4 pm itself and waited impatiently. Every second was like an hour. It had seemed an exaggeration in movies. But how true it was every time I stared at my watch. In a burst of excitement I opened the balcony door to have a glimpse of her underwear. But she had not washed any clothes. Was she equally distracted today?

The balcony door was open to brighten the room. The closed dark room was a mood dampener. When we got in the right mood it would obviously be shut. I would have liked to see her full naked glory in bright light. A tube light in a drab room made it gloomy as well. But it didn't matter. Our uncontrollable passion was enough to forget our surroundings. I sprayed deodorant on myself to heighten the effect. I had changed into a T-shirt and cargo shorts for ease. Why spend more time on nitty gritty?

Because I was on high alert, sounds that I had not previously paid attention to were audible. The faint murmurs in the courtyard, doors closing, utensils clanging, squeals from the little girl. Finally, after what felt like eternity, I heard the main door close. I waited with bated breath. Then I heard slow, soft footsteps on the wooden staircase. What was on her mind as she took each step? They didn't seem hesitant – just softly tread to avoid making a sound. Surprisingly, it had a sense of purpose. Had she done this before? Had there been other men before me? Did it matter? Not really. As long as we got what we wanted from each other. She was not mine to be possessive about.

The unlocked door opened. She entered silently with that signature gaze. The room being small, within two steps she was near the bed. I gestured towards it courteously, "Please sit."

You can't ask her to lie down straight away, can you? My mind had decided to join in.

She sat demurely, looking down, wondering how to get this started. She knew what she had come here for. She knew the boundaries she had crossed and the ones she was going to. It must be difficult, even for those who frequently found themselves in such situations.

I hoped it wouldn't take too much time to get comfortable. The countdown to the deadline had begun. It would either end with satisfaction in each other's arms or bitter interruption by the elderly couple's return.

I sat at the other end of the bed hoping my hard-on was not apparent. The thick cargo shorts was a good decision. I didn't want to show my desperation which was at its limit. The excitement increased as she relaxed and got comfortable in my presence. She sat carelessly without being conscious. She was sending the right signals.

Daylight from the balcony shone on her full body. Familiar with her clothes by now, I could imagine the underwear she wore underneath. It was getting difficult to maintain cool civility. I waited for her to make the first move.

"Hope everything is comfortable here," she began with a shy smile. Since I spoke the local language we could talk effortlessly without searching for words.

"Yes. It's good," I smiled in return. No point prolonging small talk with long sentences.

The *sari* was getting careless in its duty. Her deep navel was compressed in the folds of the small paunch. We were slowly trudging into familiar territory.

Launch at that navel! Bury your lips in it as soon as she beckons! My mind was shouting instructions. If thoughts had a voice the whole locality would have heard!

"We are so happy that you stayed here. We are simple village folks. We didn't expect someone like you to stay at our place. It has been new experience," she continued with genuine feeling. She clasped her palms together. The posture boosted up her perky tits. I could see the small cleavage promising big pleasures.

Oh when will she get to the point? Hope there is enough happening at the center to keep the old couple busy!

"Oh it is nothing," I replied automatically. "I'm also having a good stay. The whole family has been so good to me. Because of the comfort my work is going well too."

"I feel so nice to hear this. We didn't expect you to stay here for long, you know? We thought you would realise your mistake after a few days and move to the lodge. After all, you are used to better comforts in the city."

"Well….. cities do have more facilities. But then there are more bad things too. Every place has its good and bad. It is up to us to find a balance."

Why the fuck are you talking philosophy? This is not the time to reach for the soul!

"Yes. That is so right." She was impressed by the lofty reply. "You are such a good man. You have made a deep impression on all of us. I knew there was something about you." That look and that smile again.

She is complimenting me a lot. Is that the signal?

It was a bit weak as verbal signs went. But the visual signs were loud as a hoarding. She arced to adjust sitting on the rough bed. Her navel had widened to 'what- the-fuck- are-you-waiting-for'. The *pallu* slipped a little more and the blouse stretched. It exposed the top of one of her small round breasts. Wasn't she wearing a bra? She stared at the floor gentling rocking herself. She was wrestling with something on her mind. Was this the final moment of hesitation before the plunge?

There was silence in the room.

What is this? Pre - foreplay?

Did her self-preservation instincts want me to make the first move? Or was the man expected to take the lead?

The impasse was finally ended by her. "Thank you for agreeing to meet me. I have wanted to speak with you for so long but never got a chance."

Let's not waste time talking! Let's take the damn chance!

My mind was beseeching her, wishing there was telepathy between us apart from sexual tension.

Just take the call you teasing bimbo!

She looked up at me. I was staring unabashedly at her tits and navel and couldn't stop. But she didn't seem to notice. She spoke in a soft voice, "I want to talk about what's in my heart. It is very important. I hope you will understand."

Yes! Whatever! Finish with the bloody script you've prepared to appease your conscience. Let's get into it! Fast!

I was worried about losing my self- control.

Aah! I want to strip you naked! Feel every part of you! I want to –

"I want to talk about my daughter. My little girl."

What the fuck!!? Did I hear right?

My racy thoughts stopped abruptly. I was bewildered. Seeing my confusion she assumed it was because she had spoken hastily.

"Please hear me out," she cajoled with a look that could have been either yearning or pleading. But now I wasn't sure. I nodded in permission. What could I do anyway?

My face relaxed. But I sat in numb attentiveness. She heaved in relief and spoke with feeling.

"You've seen how simple the people are here. How simple life is in our village. But even we know that there is a big world out there. TV is a big part of our lives, so you can imagine. When people of high status like you-" I began to protest but she went on.

"No, No. Don't be modest. For us you are of a higher status. When people like you come to our small village we become even more aware of possibilities that exist outside. And our insignificant position in this world is reinforced. The villages around are a universe in itself. It is a source of happiness and sadness. Spoken and unspoken norms affect everyone. These matter the most to those who choose to stay or can't move out."

She looked down at her hands wondering how to come to the point. Her body still beckoned but I sensed the change. The allure of the breasts and the navel seemed to fade. Something else was emerging as the sexual ripples diminished. I tried to make sense of the vibes.

"My daughter is very precious to me. The most important thing in my life," she continued. The gaze now had a warmth and strength that was in contrast to the petite frame. This was no ignorant village woman.

"Woman's progress one hears about has still to reach all corners of the world. Even the brightest flame does not light every corner of the room equally. Especially the areas blocked by objects. Our villages are like that in some ways.

When you started talking to my daughter in English we all found it funny. It was a playful joke between both of you. We didn't pay any attention to it. Even now no one in the family thinks much about it. They are happy with the attention that their little one is getting. Except me. Because I care. Because only I understand. Because I'm unlike them in many ways.

I realised over the months that the daily talks were more than just fun. I noticed how you were as happy teaching her English as she was in learning it. You are a man with the typical qualities of a man. I know that. But you are also more than just that. You want to add value to my daughter by teaching her English. An opportunity that she will never get here."

I sat stunned realising what the conversation was all about. I wanted her to speak her heart out. But I was also hoping against hope that she wouldn't say what I feared she would. Now, even if she was stark naked with her legs spread apart I wouldn't be aroused. The moment had gone. In its place was a deep sinking feeling in my heart.

On seeing my face fall she pleaded, "Please don't take this any other way. It's only for the good. Let me explain.

My daughter is very intelligent. She grasps things very fast as you know. She is the cleverest in her nursery class. She picked up your English words easily and looked forward to more. After a few months, I realised that you were genuinely interested in helping her learn. But what good will it do to my poor girl?

You see, in our community the girls are not encouraged to study. They believe that by studying too much she would not be a good wife or a good daughter-in-law. Whether we can afford the studies is a different matter altogether. If it was a boy it might have been considered. We would have even encouraged him to sit with you and learn. What to do? The world is still the same underneath all the new. My husband has only studied till school level. And I only till primary level. Would a college girl have married my husband?

The future of my little girl, like most girls here is already set. She will be groomed to be a wife, a caretaker and a mother. She will be de-groomed to be anything else. She will study up to primary school if she is lucky. At the earliest opportunity, she will be married off. She will no longer be our responsibility. It will be up to her own self to be happy.

"I know my daughter. She is so much like me. She finds happiness on her own. In the smallest of things. She is smart enough to need just a nudge. Your English teachings ignite the passion to learn more. And that is what I am scared of. You will go sowing a seed of aspiration. And what will happen later? What if she develops a yearning to learn? What will happen when she realises that she is not supposed to grow? How will she face the truth that the only road for her leads to a house just like this one?"

Her eyes were wet though she did her best not to cry. "Please heed my request without feeling hurt. I respect your intentions but please …."

Her voice faltered but she carried on with increasing momentum.

"Please don't teach my daughter English. Please don't raise her to a level from which she will have to fall. I know it is cruel to wish this for my own daughter.

They say it is painful not to have dreams in life. And that it hurts to have unfulfilled dreams. But do you know the pain of a dream that gets crushed? And when it is crushed not because the dream is wrong but it is the wrong person having the dream? I don't want my daughter to have hopes or dreams. Let her live the life of a nobody."

She scoffed at no one in particular. "Yes sure, there are rebellious girls who defy all odds and make it big. And there are parents who stand by their child and make it happen. I have seen movies about such things. So what? How many such extraordinary stories among millions? People applaud the few who rebel against the system. But how many want to change the system so that no one needs to rebel? We all can't be super human. For some of us it takes super efforts just to be a simple human."

She made me promise again that I would not talk to her little girl in English. She got up to leave. Her *sari* was disheveled even more by her agitated state. But she didn't care. Neither did I. All I saw was a young mother doing what she thought best to keep her daughter from the heartaches of life.

It is strange how events leave their mark on your psyche. After an earthquake some see loss of lives, some see loss of property, some see an environmental disaster. And someone sees a plot for a movie.

I had two regrets in the time spent in that small village. I hadn't expected any regrets in the first place - so that was bad itself. The regret about the presumed missed chance with the woman didn't stay for too long. Nor did it hurt. The situation had been too multi- layered to figure it out. I let it go.

But the regret about the little girl stayed. Longer than I had expected it to. Something in me would be triggered whenever I saw her kind of girls. It would hurt inside. But far greater would be cautiousness in wanting to make a difference in their lives.

I was very wary of watering a plant lest someone pluck it in its infancy just because they didn't want it to flower.

The Pickpocket

The lady was focused only on her designer dress. She was trying to avoid the dirt on the road. The jostling crowd was less important in comparison. A bulky handbag dangled precariously from sleeveless shoulders. Men walked closer to see more of what was on show. Suddenly, she felt a sharp tug on her shoulders. Her limits stopped at glances and didn't extend to touch. She flared up in anger. As she turned around to give the offender a piece of her mind a shocking realisation hit her. The centre of attraction had been her handbag and not her! But before she could scream in alarm, the handbag had melted into the crowd, leaving its strap behind as a souvenir of the bitter evening.

He moved swiftly but casually through the crowd. He was careful not to run - an office executive late for work. The handbag was in his knapsack which had a logo of a respectable MNC. He walked towards a small alley parallel to the main market road. Slowing down he turned into a narrow street which led to yet another road. There was no commotion behind. The mission had been successful. Relief and euphoria came out as a deep release of breath.

He slipped into an old grey Fiat parked on the road and drove off.

Few more then it's good to go. Another month or so. Then I will meet Bhai. Thoughts raced to use up the adrenalin still running in him.

In the course of the day, he made four more successful strikes. With two purses and two wallets, it had been a good day at work. Unlike his views about life, he viewed his performance in black and white. If you went for the kill you had to make the kill. In his opinion, escaping when caught in the act was a black mark too. It showed gap in skill or misjudgment of a target.

The pickpocket operated in middle class suburbs of a vibrant city. People in this stretched city were always engrossed in activity. When idle they were lost in their thoughts. The vagaries of trying to lead a successful life made most of them vulnerable and stressed. Unless robbed unaware, only a handful would make half-hearted attempts to chase the thief. People were reluctant to give chase. Going to the police was an additional hassle. In a city where murders and break-ins were common, where did a pickpocketing case stand? And instead of sympathy, they would be admonished for their carelessness.

His modus operandi of escape had been time tested over the years. On rare occasions, it even involved standing among the useless crowd of onlookers. There were always people to witness the victim's plight, thankful it wasn't them instead. His chief getaway method was to dissolve into the crowd by walking away casually. He would never run. He would have parked a non-descript car in a nearby street - the car borrowed from his mechanic friend. On days he worked a railway station, the best bet was to catch a train from the next platform. Good Samaritans, if any, would be looking for a shabby rogue fleeing. Not a well-dressed young man who had been present there and was now not around.

This unique pickpocket handled his profession very professionally. Not for him was the greed or the need of grabbing every opportunity. He was in no rush to amass lots of money. The stereotyped version in movies was 'one last crime to last a lifetime'. It was in his opinion, non-existent and dangerous. A habitual petty thief was like a gambler. The thrill of the catch was as exhilarating as the money itself. And with every win it got harder to quit. So why risk it for one big haul when you know that you will do it again? 'Smaller the pick, softer the kick' was what he lived by.

He used his knowledge of psychology, profiling, body language and other relevant parameters to choose his victim. He envisioned the reactions of the target. He mapped out escape routes. He thought of worst case scenarios and his way out of them. Unlike petty pickpockets, he never marked the target on the size of the prize nor ease of the hit.

Deceit not dagger was the weapon of his choice. He was fully aware that he was committing a crime. But it was the least harmful among all, wasn't it? He didn't resort to violence nor burgle anyone's house. The sleight of hand was his forte. It was his skill against the victim's presence of mind. Finders keepers. If he could find a way to the wallets and not get caught, then it was his to keep.

His 'good boy' looks was an effective mask to fool the public. Appearance and upbringing were great assets. In this city of superficial external profiles, persona was everything. Movies and public perception had set an image of what a pickpocket looked like. The fact that most did fit the profile made him even more unique.

Though in his twenties, one could mistake him for a college student. His medium height helped not stand out in a crowd. He was fair – a huge factor in this colour biased society. His well-built body was maintained through regular exercise. This need for physical fitness was not vanity driven. It had been a necessity growing up in the harsh slums. It later became a resource in the field. He could outrun the crowd if the situation arose. In event of a rare occurrence (which thankfully had not yet come) he could handle at least two men at a time.

He was always meticulously dressed - never shabby but never ever loud. His formal attire was ironed trousers, shirt with formal shoes. Casual dressing consisted of jeans, a collared T- shirt with a pocket and sneakers. The clothes were rip offs of well-known brands. He could afford to buy originals of some brands. But why waste money if the only purpose was to make a point? In his knapsack was a pair of sunglasses, spectacles, a cap and a jacket to change his profile instantly if needed.

This polished approach to life could be traced to his upbringing.

In the slums of the city, contact with nefarious characters was unavoidable. Slums were a common refuge for the marginalised and a thus an ideal breeding ground for the antisocial. Circumstances and proximity to such elements made this transformation smooth.

The riffraff in his slum were mostly involved in petty crime. He stayed well clear of the few involved in hard crime. He had never been fascinated by the high life of crime. Like most people living in the gutters of society, all he wanted was what he saw others have - a decent family, steady money and respect. He had gotten none.

He grew up listening to the boasts of conquests by petty thieves and con men of his slum. As part of a select group of kids he was taught the tricks of the pickpocket trade. This was fun for the innocent boys, not knowing that they were being groomed for the future. They practiced their skills after school and on holidays. The 'classroom' was usually an area away from their home base. At first there were dummy bags to practice on. Later, pockets of their own slum were picked and dutifully returned intact. In the early stages of the resident target practice, these novice pickpockets would always get caught but be sent off with only a rap. What they were being trained for was an open secret and no one minded. The adage 'crime does not pay' sounded hollow to those who earned a pitiful amount through honest living.

These activities though were kept secret from his mother who strongly disapproved of it. She had loftier dreams for him. Fortunately for him, she worked six days a week at a factory and was away most of the day.

A select few among the young recruits graduated to skilled youngsters - fully aware of their deeds. Relieving people of their valuables became an outlet for getting back at the society which belittled them. The plight of the victims, supposedly better off, gave them a sense of superiority. The booty was shared between the upper hierarchy, the local leadership and the pickpocket.

The formative days of pickpocketing had made a deep impression on the young lad. Once on being caught, he had been slapped around with a good dose of abuses. Then, to his surprise he had been let off. At another instance, just as he was about to make a grab for the bag the man had become alert and rushed ahead with a warning glare. The young pickpocket learnt that a victim's reaction would be a mixture of confusion, self-preservation and anger. The victim was more worried about the loss of important items like IDs, monthly travel pass and cards than the actual money. They would be relieved, even feel fortunate, if by any chance the only loss was that of money. And no one wanted to add to their stress by taking a pickpocket through the hassles of justice. Life in this cruel world had taught bystanders to mind their own business. These insights convinced him that if he was ever to have a career of crime, pickpocketing would be the chosen sector.

But he had no intention of doing so when he was growing up.

Right from childhood he knew that he was different from the rest of the kids. He was a misfit in looks. He had features attributed to a well-bred lineage. He had not known his father. There was no photo of him either. His mother never talked about him nor encouraged that line of conversation. All she said was that his father was dead. Sometimes he suspected that she almost added 'to us'. They had moved to the slums when he was a baby. His mother worked in the nearby factory where women were employed to stitch clothes for export. Since she kept her private life private and was social only as much as required, people around could only speculate on her past life.

He had grown up on gossip and taunts. On cruel days, he was said to be a bastard child of a rich man where his mother must have worked as a maid. The sleazier version was that he was an inevitable result of a bar dancer servicing wealthy patrons. On sad days, he was the symbol of tragic love between a rich man and a poor woman torn apart by society. On sympathetic days, he was from a good family fallen on hard times after the husband's death. And on rare days, he was a diamond in the coal mine waiting for his true destiny to be unraveled. But no matter the day, this good looking boy was the proverbial black sheep of the slum.

His mother's relentless determination to instill in him high aspirations made him a misfit in outlook too. This reinforced the speculation of his mother's background. But she cared not for what the world thought of her and her son. She always encouraged him to believe beyond the obvious. While others went to school half-heartedly knowing there was no future for them, he studied with an aim to move to a better place in life. His mother knew that she could not insulate him from the anti- social elements in the slum. Instead of fighting a fruitless cause, she tried balancing the negative associations with positive reinforcements. Whenever she could, his mother bought him books - not toys or sweets. He was dressed like any other kid in a middle class household. The clothes were either discards from the affluent or cheap imitations. No matter what, it matched up to the best of the lot in style. She filled his mind with possibilities of a better life that education brought. Whenever possible she took him to see the better side of life in the city. Her conversations would be peppered with motivational insights. "There is value in everything. One has to have the wisdom to see it," she preached. "Doesn't the rag-picker make money from waste? Don't tramps survive on garbage? The same flower that is outside our slum will look more beautiful in a rich flat." The die was being cast.

The unexpected demise of his mother forced him to abandon his studies midway through college. His mother's wish to see him graduate remained a dream. But the seed of learning was firmly ingrained. Life became his lifelong teacher. Life would bestow degrees as he advanced.

It's not as if he hadn't tried to live an honest life, earning his livelihood the straight way. Unable to complete his graduation and having no backing, the only jobs offered were the daily wage kind. His mind raised to a higher level by good upbringing was not reflected in reality and how the world saw him. It was hard adjusting his aspirations with society's expectations. The mould that his mother had sought to cast him in was slowly crumbling. What hurt him was the way people associated the work with the worker. Working as an errand boy or a labourer was not as bad as the treatment received because of it. They were judged in entirety and not as individuals. Those at the bottom of the workforce were just means to an end.

It irked him that the affluent also displayed mentality that society only associated with the lowly mass. What good then was education and family background? At least people like him had an excuse for such behaviour.

Grinding through the early years to earn honest bread, he tried his best to resist the temptation of pickpocketing. But it was ever present in the background urging him to make it his life. Hanging out with childhood pals who had branched into petty crimes was no help. He found it increasingly difficult to justify not following their path. Words like 'freedom', 'master of own life' 'any time money' were showered during conversations. 'Steal the valuables of those who don't value us', 'more money for less efforts',' short life but grand life' were lofty slogans thrown at him over drinks. Somewhere in his heart these resonated through the day as he slogged as a lowly worker. Years of conditioning in the slums could not be washed away so easily.

No matter if a donkey had it in it to win a horse race. No one would give it a break because they only saw a beast of burden. And even if given a chance, who would want to see a donkey run among graceful horses?

When he finally secured a job as an office boy in a good corporate office he resolved to discard the blanket of self- doubt and get off the slippery path. But it turned out to be the final straw - the opening of the last bolt, into a world of petty crime.

To cut a long revelation short, he realized to his disappointment that thieving existed in society in different forms. It spanned class, education, money and gender. People didn't call it stealing and in some cases it wasn't even considered as one. It ranged from pilfering of office stationary to inflating of expenses. At the upper end of this cultured robbery was siphoning of funds and fiddling of accounts.

Finding this mindset among the well – off made him lose faith in the values espoused so often. This was not what his mother had believed in when she urged him to be a part of a better society. No one was above the lure of easy money. Not everyone stole nor did they do it all the time. But the undeniable truth was that everyone from the top boss to the lowest worker was capable of doing so. Rank, role, richness, was no deterrent to those who sought an opportunity. In his office a few top managers had made money on the side through official channels. That it was an open secret but no one dared point a finger astounded him. Such was life that the scapegoats for the conscience keepers were the low end staff. They were regarded as the ones more likely to cheat and pilfer.

There was a distant cousin of thieving which society accepted grudgingly. People committed it without a second thought. Some actually derived pleasure out of it. Almost everyone had done it knowingly or unknowingly at some point in their lives. It lay between stealing and borrowing. In India it was called *'dhaapna'* - borrowing and not returning it. Conveniently slipping out of the borrower's mind. It ranged from expensive tools to common items like books, pen, stapler etc. (Ask anyone the grief of a lost pen.) It was never money because that would cross the line into the darker shades of grey.

Once he made up his mind to lead the life of a pickpocket he decided to be the best. He worked on it like an artist would on his art. It would be his career and not a means of livelihood. He set rules, tactics and progressions for the future. He believed in the art of pickpocket and not just the act of it. Like a self-employed person he worked on improving his skills and increasing opportunities.

After a few years of mining the streets, he realised that though he would always be a pickpocket till he could physically manage it, he needed a platform for stability. There had to be more to him than a petty thief. Climbing the ladder of crime was not for him. He was happy being an invisible small fish in a big pond. He learnt from the world that respectability was an ideal mask for unrespectable deeds. His goal thereafter was to secure a respectable front. This make-believe society judged a book only by its cover.

'Bhai' meaning elder brother was a term of respect, common among the city's underworld. There were major 'Bhais' and minor 'Bhais'. The local head honcho, the Bhai he knew since childhood, controlled their slum on behalf of a bigger don. He had often requested *Bhai* to help set up a small business of his own but was laughed off. However he kept it up whenever he chanced upon the *Bhai*. In the world of crime, pickpockets had no real respect. Their deeds didn't have the heady mixture of danger, machoism and big bucks. A couple of years and many attempts later, when he was considered ready by their standards, he was offered a proposition.

In a not so busy street, *Bhai* had a small shop lying vacant. Not much could be done with it due to space constraint. Such shops lay in the legal grey zone and could only exist with an understanding with the right officials. He was offered that shop on a nominal rent. He planned to set up a Xerox business or something along those lines. What was important was his image makeover to that of a respectable person. The details of the business could be sorted out later. He knew that the shop though his for all practical purposes, would be indirectly controlled by *Bhai*. It would be a conduit for shady dealings if needed. But that didn't matter as he had no choice anyways.

The whole deal cost Rs.2 lakhs. He had kept aside money for such an endeavor over the years. Each haul of his had been divided into expenses, savings, investment and pleasure. It had not been easy. After all he robbed pockets, not banks and houses. How much did people carry with them anyways? And with the growing popularity of cards, the money in a wallet was shrinking. Still, there were places where people preferred carrying cash. The skill was in spotting them. There were hot spots in the city where money flowed like water. And there were those who bought luxury items with wads of money. How else would black money be spent if not through cash?

The day finally arrived when he had the money to seal the contract. There had been regular informal talks between the seasoned pickpocket and the *Bhai's* contact to gauge his seriousness. Finally, he was instructed to visit an office on a given date to complete the formalities. The office was in a distant suburb of the city. It served as the respectable front for *Bhai's* nefarious activities. The money had to be handed in cash. In their world deals were sealed by cash and word of honour. A man who reneged on his word was as good as dead. So either you gave your word or you didn't get into such conversations.

The well-dressed pickpocket casually held the bag containing his hard earned money as he entered the narrow market street. It was an ordinary cloth bag, not worth looking at twice. Bags attracted attention if it was bulky, flashy or held too protectively by the owner. So he made no big deal of his bag. He was just another guy on his way somewhere.

The sun shining pleasantly on a cool early evening mirrored the young man's mood. He had a profound sense of an approaching milestone. The air was filled with beseeching voices as shouts interspersed with one another. People milled about as if they had nowhere to go. There were always people on the road in this overpopulated city. An empty street signaled a dead end or a place to avoid.

He walked steadily studying the crowd. It came naturally to him. Crowds pleased him. They were like trees to a bird - sustenance and shelter. Crowds meant money and avenues of escape.

A young woman with an appealing figure walked ahead of the cheerful pickpocket. He watched her in his professional mode. There was a time and place for personal and professional instincts. Her expensive top with tight hip hugging jeans attracted appreciative glances. He wondered why she was walking in a packed narrow street. He presumed she was heading for the expensive boutiques at the end of the road.

A little boy held her hand. One tended to go easy on people with children. But along with the elderly, those with small kids were the easiest targets. The immediate concern in distress situations would be the safety of the child. The victim would not dash behind the thief. It was an unfair world. Who would know it better than him? The opportunity sauntering ahead was pretty tempting and an easy one at that. Lone rich woman with a kid in a crowded street was a neon sign flashing 'Welcome!'

He was suddenly in two minds. Should he go for it and meet *Bhai* tomorrow? Or should he take a different route to the office a few hours after his getaway? His professional instinct had automatically got into gear. But he knew that it was too risky. The office was just round the corner. It would be too close to the drama. Today his priorities were different. He sighed aloud to let go the pull of the catch.

Was it worth throwing away the persistence of so many years just for this? The answer was an easy one. He rued the missed chance as he appraised the swinging hips and the swinging handbag. Today would be some lucky bastard's day. Worse - there would be no one to take the opportunity. He walked slowly wanting to stay behind her as much as possible. Like flower to a bee, he was unable to break away from the lure of what could have been an easy catch. The end of the street opened into a crossroad. The road straight ahead would be her destination. He had to take a right for *Bhai's* office.

As they neared the end of the road he sighed again in resignation. The junction was jam packed. People emerged from four directions and tried to go in a hundred. With self-righteous 'right-of-passage' cycles squeezed through the teeming mass as their owners walked beside it. These people believed that their cycles did not classify as vehicles because it didn't have engines. The zone was pickpocket heaven. With the despair of a seasoned thief he got closer to the woman for a final glance at the vanishing prospect. The crowd converging at the crossroad pushed past hurriedly, eager to get out of the jam. Women tried not to give much thought to the unavoidable physical brushes. As he watched, the petite woman was swallowed by the mass. Her one hand clutched that large expensive handbag and the other dragged the helpless kid.

After a few minutes of jostling and pushing he managed to wrest himself free. *What a waste.* He kept muttering in his mind. *It's OK. There'll always be more in the future. Today, it's only about finalising this deal. I hope there are not many conditions. I want to set it all up in a week and get back to my routine.*

Walking a few metres further, he saw the building which housed *Bhai's* office. The signboard outside read 'B. Group of Companies'. It didn't specify the 'group' or what 'companies' they kept. But the office looked respectable enough from outside. Image was what mattered after all.

As he approached the office, a deep realisation dawned on him like a cold sharp sword through the heart. It was followed by the chilled feeling of ice water poured down his back. He stopped dead in his tracks. He knew! He just knew it then. But he was too shocked to verify it. He wanted the thumping in his heart to reduce to a bearable level. Within a minute or two he started walking again, dragging his steps. Life had showered enough disappointments. What was one more? The lightness of the bag was verification in itself. But he slid his hand in to confirm what he already knew.

He had been robbed. The money had been slipped out from a deep cut in the cloth bag. He had been so sure of the ordinariness of the bag that he had forgotten another major factor of choosing a target. The target himself! His looks and his attire matched the profile of the affluent. His asset as a pickpocket had worked against him outside the role. While he had been engrossed watching the woman, someone or a group, had set sights on him. The pickpocket had become the pickpocketed! The predator had been preyed by his own kind.

A sudden massive wave of despair and rage washed over him. All he had now was a shattered dream. He would have to begin from scratch. He would have to save money all over again. He would have to wait for another shot at respectability. He tried not to think of how many years that would take. The intense feeling subsided as quickly as it had risen. And then he couldn't help laughing at the irony of it all. While his 'lost opportunity' had been walking ahead of him someone had not lost an opportunity. Such was life. And life went on. Another lesson learnt the hard way. Another valuable experience in his quest to be the best in his field.

When he reached the building he did not stop. He walked on, maintaining his stride and soothing his pride. The office and his dream were left behind. For the time being.

Final thoughts

I wrote the first complete drafts of a few of these stories more than 20 years ago when I was a youngster. I was a student at an engineering college in a town away from my home in Mumbai. I wrote stories to keep alive my love for writing and as a better way to deal with homesickness. I typed the stories (originally written in long hand using a ballpoint pen on faded paper) just to preserve them. Brushing up my writing skills (however amateur), I added a few more stories and polished the old ones. I wonder if the reader can detect which stories bear the mark of a young guy and which bear that of someone way past that mark.

Most fiction is based on reworked facts. The characters and events in this book are fictionalized by my perception and imagination.

Prudence dictates that professional help be taken. But the entire process of writing, editing, designing the cover page (Picture courtesy Unsplash & Pixabay) and self-publishing was exciting and enlightening.

I am aware of my limitations as an author. All mistakes are mine alone whether technical or content-wise. If you do notice any, please help me make the book better by emailing the error to me at inishantk@gmail.com. Feedback on the book is always welcome.

Nishant Kumta

Printed in Great Britain
by Amazon